TONY N' WEDDING

by ARTIFICIAL INTELLIGENCE

CONCEIVED BY

NANCY CASSARO

CREATED BY

THOMAS MICHAEL ALLEN,
JAMES ALTUNER, MARK CAMPBELL,
NANCY CASSARO, PATRICIA CREGAN,
ELIZABETH DENNEHY,
CHRISTOPHER FRACCHIOLLA,
JACK FRIS, KEVIN A. LEONIDAS,
MARK NASSAR, LARRY PELLEGRINI,
SUSAN VARON and MOIRA WILSON

Originally Produced by
Joseph and Daniel Corcoran
in association with Artificial Intelligence

SAMUEL FRENCH, INC.
45 WEST 25TH STREET   NEW YORK 10010
7623 SUNSET BOULEVARD HOLLYWOOD 90046
LONDON   TORONTO

IMPORTANT BILLING AND CREDIT REQUIREMENTS

All producers of TONY N' TINA'S WEDDING *must* give credit to the Owners, as sole Authors of the Play, in all programs distributed in connection with performances of the Play and in all instances in which the title of the Play appears for purposes of advertising, publicizing or otherwise exploiting the Play and/or a production thereof, including, without limitation, posters, souvenir books and playbills. The names of the Owners *must* also appear immediately following the title of the Play, and *must* appear in size of type not less than fifty percent (50%) the size of type used for the title. The above billing *must* appear as follows:

TONY N' TINY'S WEDDING by Artificial Intelligence. Conceived by Nancy Cassaro. Originally created by Thomas Allen, James Altuner, Mark Campbell, Nancy Cassaro, Patricia Cregan, Elizabeth Dennehy, Christopher Fracchiolla, Jack Fris, Kevin Leonidas, Mark Nassar, Larry Pellegrini, Susan Varon and Moira Wilson. Originally produced by Joseph Corcoran and Daniel Corcoran in association with Artificial Intelligence.

Tony 'n' Tina's Wedding officially opened on February 20, 1988. It was originally produced by Joseph Corcoran and Daniel Corcoran in association with Artificial Intelligence at Washington Square Church, 135 West Fourth Street; reception at Carmelita's Restaurant, 150 East 14th Street, New York City with the following cast:

Valentina Lynne Vitale	Nancy Cassaro
Tony Nunzio	Mark Nassar
Barry Wheeler	Mark Campbell
Connie Mocogni	Moira Wilson
Dominic Fabrizzi	James Altuner
Donna Marsala	Elizabeth Dennehy
Johnny Nunzio	Eli Ganias
Marina Galino	Patricia Cregan
Josephina Vitale	Susan Varon
Luigi Domenico	Jay Harran
Joey Vitale	Thomas Michael Allen
Rose Domenico	Jennifer Heftler
Sr. Albert Maria	Elizabeth Herring
Tony Nunzio Sr.	Christopher Fracchiolla
Madeline Monroe	Jennie Moreau
Grandma Nunzio	Denise Moses
Michael Just	Jack Fris
Father Mark	Phil Rosenthal
Sal Antonucci	Vincent Floriani
Vinnie Black	Kevin A. Leonidas
Loretta Black	Joanna Cocca
Nicki Black	Judy Sheehan
Timmy Sullivan	Tom Hogan
Donny Dulce	Michael Winther
Celeste Romano	Kia Colton
Carlo Cannoli	Charlie Terrat
Rocco Caruso	Towner Gallaher

Directed by Larry Pellegrini
Choreography by Hal Simons
Costumes, hair and make-up by Juan de Armas
Set Direction by Randall Thropp

iv

TABLE OF CONTENTS

Nancy Cassaro wishes to thank
the following people:

Dr. and Mrs. James P. Cassaro,
Tony Dowdy, John Goffredo,
Teresa Hagar, Joanne Hastings,
Stephen Holden, Richard Krawetz,
David Rothenberg, George Sheanshang,
Gary Schneider, Bruce Schwarz, and
Carolyn Scott.

CHARACTERS

CAST BREAKDOWN FOR
TONY 'N' TINA'S WEDDING

TONY – groom, mid 20's, handsome, rowdy, charming.

TINA – bride, mid 20's, pretty, party girl, headstrong, tough.

BARRY – best man, late 20's, everybody's pal, drug dealer.

CONNIE – maid of honor, late 20's, pregnant, jaded.

DOMINIC – usher, mid 20's, party animal with a heart of gold.

DONNA – bridesmaid, mid 20's, cute white trash, good singer.

JOHNNY – usher, 20, Tony's little brother. A cute flirt.

MARINA – bridesmaid, mid 20's, insecure tag-along, the gang's doormat.

JOSEPHINA – Tina's mom, 45, strong willed, overweight, a martyr.

LUIGI – Tina's great uncle, late 70's, old world gentleman, speaks Italian (can be played by a younger actor).

JOEY – Tina's brother, 30, gay, loves "show biz," not flamboyant .

SISTER ALBERT MARIA – Tina's cousin, mid 20's, family oddball.

TONY NUNZIO SR. – Tony's dad, 50, charismatic in a sleazy way, sees himself as a king.

MADELINE MONROE – Tony Sr.'s girlfriend, 20's, stripper, good looking and hard living.

GRANDMA NUNZIO – Tony's grandma, 70's, spry, a little crazy. (Grandma Nunzio can be played by a younger actor as well.)

MICHAEL JUST – late 20's, Tina's ex-boyfriend, just got out of rehab, a burnout.

FATHER MARK – priest, 30's, thinks he's hip and one of the gang.

SAL ANTONUCCI – photographer, 40, pushy, eccentric, bored with his job.

VINNIE BLACK – caterer, late 40's, amateur comedian, used car salesman type.

LORETTA BLACK – Vinnie's wife, late 40's, brow beaten by Vinnie, a little worn.

DONNY DULCE – late 20's, sexy leader of the wedding band. Excellent pop singer.

cont.

CELESTE ROMANO – keyboard player and vocalist for the wedding band. Trampy but attractive.

RICK DeMARCO – 20's, hired to videotape wedding, Joey's boyfriend. (In the original company this character was known as Timmy Sullivan.)

Also needed: Bass player and drummer—must not be afraid to act.

TINA VITALE

"Happy birthday Tina," the children shouted. Tina knelt on the chair pushed up close to the yellow formica kitchen table, her chin almost touching the four tiny flames that burnt atop the cake. "Make a wish! Make a wish!" the children cried. Tina glanced at her mom, who nodded as if to say,"It's your day, Tina, your wish will come true." Tina looked at her gifts: a huge pile of wonder, all for her. She looked at the faces of her friends, delighted, laughing, smeared with ice cream and cake and candy—things forbidden except on special days. She was the cause of it all. She made her wish, and opened her eyes. Amidst the smoke from the candles, the kids clapping, and another ragged verse of "Happy Birthday," she heard her mom say, "Tina, starting today you're a big girl. This is a big day." At that moment, the true nature of life became clear to Tina. Life was little bunches of time leading up to Big Days—days distinguished by gifts, parties and transformation.

Whether a graduation or a wake, a New Year's Eve or an after-prom, Big Days always carried the promise that a new phase of life was about to begin for Tina. But as the years went by, Big Days began to bring little new for Tina but a fresh determination never to drink again. Worse, Big Days had begun to be accompanied by little dreads as they hinted that maybe her life was hopelessly stuck. But then Tony proposed. Not that Tina needed Tony. The years had also seen her grow into a self-sufficient, bull-headed young woman, always able to hold her own. But she had adopted a credo: "Know what you want, Know how to get it, and Look good getting it"—and she wanted Tony. So as the sea gulls proved to Columbus that the New World was just over the horizon, Tony's proposal catapulted Tina to the brink of the Biggest Day—the Freshest Start—of her life.

For Tina, walking up the aisle, taking her vows, and even the kiss are primarily for her mother and the photographer. The true ceremony is the bacchanal of wild dancing, uncontrolled drinking and voracious eating that comes after the "I do's" are done. It is a whirling dervish affair that spins and spins with a life of it's own until the moment when she and Tony, a waltzing blur of white, laden with gifts, are transported through the magic marriage vortex into the clouds of their new life. But unexpected strings are holding Tina back. Tina's father is there, defined by his absence. Her sadness is his date for the evening. Her mother is giggling with Tony's father. It's clear that Tina isn't the only one who is changing. And Michael, pale and sad, appears like the Creature, rising up from the swamp of all that she used to be, a slimy hand gripping the hem of her gown. She should be emerging like a butterfly from the cocoon, but she is earthbound, drowning in a bellyful of booze, anger, and disappointment. Where is the New Life? Then she sees Tony. He stands like a lighthouse on the battered shores of her ceremony. Starting today ... This is a Big Day. A trade has to be made. Something has to be left behind in this wrecked hall. She must leave everything behind—except Tony—and walk out the door.

TONY NUNZIO

One afternoon, Johnny came crying into his dad's strip joint, The Animal Kingdom. Tony had been home from school for awhile, washing up glasses and watering down the booze. Dad was down in the basement as usual, talking on the phone and drinking. "They were teasing me, Tony," Johnny sobbed. "They kept asking me where our mom was and I told them she was dead, but they just kept laughing and holding up a match." Tony topped off a bottle of Dewar's with water until the dark amber liquid turned caramel. "Did you kick their ass?" he said. "No." Johnny sobbed hard. He's not a tough kid, Tony thought. "Listen. Mom's dead. Forget about those jerky friends of yours." Tony was four when his mom left, and he can remember a little. The rest he's been able to piece together by listening to people talk around the "Kingdom"! Prostitutes, transvestites, strippers, drunks—they mutter a lot, and so does Tony's dad. Tony knew the truth. His dad and mom hated each other so much and fed the hate with so many gallons of booze that one night one of them tried to set the other on fire. But the truth is not what's important here. "Kids used to say the same stuff to me." "Really?" Johnny's eyes brightened. "Yeah. Just forget it. Mom's dead. That's it." Tony backed this pronouncement with a confident look that pierced Johnny's doubt and lightened his heart. It's good to keep a lid on some things.

Tony suddenly sits bolt upright in bed, sweating. He peers into the darkness. What a dream. He had stood in the desert looking at a scaffold in the distance. Black against the dawn, it looked like a dinosaur with an enormous head. Someone handed him a drink. "Here's to the big moment,

Doc." Tony took the glass of champagne, but could not drink. He gazed at the dreadful thing in the distance—his creation. A triumph of physics. 5 ... 4 ... 3 ... "NO!" Suddenly Tony was atop the monster. "I can't let this go on! It's my fault!" He clamped a saucepan lid on the bomb. ... 1 ... zero—flash. The world rumbled and a giant crack opened in the earth swallowing Mrs. Vitale, Rose, Dad, Johnny—Tina. They all slid by and into Hell ... what a dream. Tony looks at the glowing numbers on the bedstand clock: five a.m. Ten hours till the wedding. 9, 8, 7 ... He has spent most of his life keeping the lid on. Now he is bringing the forces of guaranteed destruction together for a wedding. If it had been up to him, he and Tina would be in the Camaro, license in hand, bound for some small town chapel where they could be married in peace. But no. "Your father isn't going to bring his little girlfriend, is he, Tony?" He is. "That Vitale woman doesn't think she's going to make a tea party out of this, does she?" She does. Thoughts come rapidly to Tony: gotta keep Dad from messing up Mrs. V's day. But it's Dad's day, too, gotta remember that. What am I, a baby-sitter? It's Tina's day! I gotta be there for her! His Day. Her Day. The Day. The thoughts gridlock as his head hits the pillow. Slowly, languidly, another thought percolates into his brain. It bobs up and down there and waves a little red flag. Finally it gets Tony's attention: Your Day. Swiftly, a big lid clamps down on the little thought, crushing it. Tony sighs.

DOMINIC FABRIZZI

Late, late one night Dominic's dad went to a union meeting at the Sausage Maker's Local 235. Nobody knows what was discussed that night, but everyone knows that Dominic's dad was a man of fierce principle who would dive headlong into any battle against all odds. They also know that pieces of his white panama hat were subsequently found in sausage grinder #5. So at ten years of age, Dom was fatherless. But he had inherited much of his dad's noble character. He proved it right away by acquiring and selling on the street anything that could bring a few bucks to support him and his mother, and later by chasing this same mother out of the house with a baseball bat when she'd had one sleazy boyfriend too many. It was this little boy bachelor living in a huge rented house that attracted the attention of Nunzio who anointed him "Son," and began paying his rent and buying his food in return for "a little work around the Animal Kingdom"— a "little work" which Dom is still doing to this day. But everyone has benefitted from the bargain. Dom found in the Animal Kingdom a place to grow up that had all the charms of Pleasure Island, and the whole Nunzio family found a friend of unstinting loyalty and devotion.

A wedding is the ultimate arena for a guy like Dominic. First of all, it's a great place to make deals; and this he does in all manner of goods from VCR's to portable phones. But a wedding is also an event of historic proportions seething with the high passion of love fulfilled, petty pastimes of old jealousies revived, and the gnashing demands of ancient animosities between clans. Dom avails himself of all this drama, drawn to it by his powerful sense of propriety and old world right and wrong. But suddenly, unexpectedly, he finds himself in the midst of a whirlwind whipped up by Sister Albert Maria. Here, he is confronted head-on with the great Battle of the Titans: Dom—Partaker of the Feast of Life vs. Dom—Champion of the Respectable Choice. The former looks at Sister and sees the great shame in turning away a woman so beautiful and so wanting, the latter sees a woman obviously married to God—or at least dressed that way. And then there's Donna who is becoming livid with jealousy and pretty vocal about it. Having been together since the third grade, Dom and Donna are past masters of the Big-Bang relationship, exploding outward with fury one moment and pulling back together with undeniable magnetism the next. But there's a terrible look in Donna's eye this time ... and a gorgeous look in Sister's eyes. It makes Dom think of his dad for a moment, and what he might have said: It's late, late at night—and for guys like us, there is a meat grinder just around the corner.

DONNA MARSALA

A star is a bright heavenly presence moving inexorably in a timeless orbit that is its destiny; and all that the star's light falls upon is forever woven into that destiny. For Donna the proof that she is the center of the universe came one afternoon back in the third grade. She had been bad—so bad that Sister Camilla kept her after school and made her kneel with bare knees on a cold linoleum floor sprinkled with hard, dry rice. Time passed, and the pain was becoming unbearable. Suddenly, someone was there. He stood in the hall, gazing through the open door at her. She slowly raised her head. Her eyes, filled with tears, met his and he was flooded by her light, pulled into her orbit, ennobled by her beauty. He rushed in, pulled her to her feet and punched the Dragon Camilla in the stomach. Before the dragon had time to recover, Donna had been swept down the steps, onto the street and into a life forever linked, forever betrothed—to Dominic.

Tina has been linked to Donna too, since before they were old enough to talk behind each other's back. She believes that Donna is definitely just a breath away from winning "Star Search"—then Beverly Hills, a chauffeur, and a prime-time salute to her career upon her untimely death. But for some reason, when it came time to choose her Maid of Honor, Tina passed right over Donna the Star. Next to the bride, the maid of honor is the most looked at person in the wedding. It's a star position! Now Donna is determined to find another way to shine. Her plan is simple: carefully follow up on some groundwork flirting she laid last month when Donny Dulce was playing at Sparks, and grab some limelight by singing a couple of songs with the band. The trouble is, while Donna knows that flirting for a gig is just business, Dominic doesn't see it that way. He sees Donna's smiling and melting and heaving great sighs all around Donny as—well, flirting. He also feels that Donna's "business" with Donny naturally clears the way for him to engage in some heavy eye contact of his own with Sister Albert Maria. Now a remarkable law of physics comes into play. A star is essentially a mass of molecules that can, with the proper trigger, be angered to greater and faster emotion. The subsequent heat and pressure then combine to create an explosion so tremendous and a field of gravity so intense that it swallows up even the star's own light. When this occurs, that lofty, magical, heavenly presence is transformed into the most terrifying force known to man—a force from which nothing can escape. Scientists call it a Black Hole. You can call it Donna.

BARRY WHEELER

Barry is a self-described "control freak" who ironically has never had his life under control. Orphaned at a very young age, Barry was sent to live with his grandma who worked as a cleaning woman at a staple factory. This left him with a lot of unsupervised days which were spent engaged in petty theft and vandalism. It also left him within walking distance of Nunzio's School for Boys—the Animal Kingdom—where he spent a lot of unsupervised nights in the bosom of select dancers therein. Unfortunately, as time went on, Barry spent fewer and fewer nights at the Kingdom, and more in jail. Which led Barry to the first real choice of his life—prison or the Army.

After his sentence in the military, Barry returned to the neighborhood a changed man. No longer would he be ripping off garages for bikes, beers or lawn mowers. It was time to get respectable. He cut his hair, rented a suburban home, moved in with Connie, and established a business as a drug dealer. In the service, Barry had learned about control—well actually, controlled substances.

Being Tony's best man is a testament to Barry's new found respectability and a test of his ability to control things. All matters pertaining to Tony must go through him. He has crafted and rehearsed a perfect toast to send the bride and groom on their voyage through life. Most importantly, he will be the sole supplier of the "party essentials" be they natural, synthetic or psychedelic, and as such he will certainly be the kingpin of the celebration. But Barry has overlooked a detail, a weak link in his chain of control, and that weak link is Michael. Everyone knows that Michael is a loose cannon and that he's not taking Tina's marrying Tony very well. Everyone also knows that Michael's on the wagon and can't handle booze or drugs of any kind. Having brought him to the wedding, Barry feels he must keep Michael from making trouble, but he's also obliged as Doctor Dope to do drugs and plenty of them. Barry figures the only way to control this situation is to keep Michael near to him, and on drugs. It's better than letting Michael wander around unsupervised. Besides, Barry's also responsible for Michael's having a good time, right? So, as the Captain of Control takes charge of the King of Chaos the question arises: who's leading whom? And on closer examination one might ask: by the way, which one's which?

TERRY, AKA SISTER ALBERT MARIA

Terry doesn't look like a turdball, in fact, she has always been pretty. But as Tina will tell you—and she is the expert—looks have nothing to do with Turdballness. Turdballness is a personality trait, a state of mind, a geeky, faggy way of doing things that makes coolness an impossible dream. But Terry wasn't just any old turdball, she was full of complexities and hence unpredictable. She always admired Tina, and this admiration grew by leaps and bounds when Tina began to prove her coolness by drinking in parking lots, making out in parking lots and throwing up in parking lots. This aroused in Terry a powerful desire to follow in the footsteps of her cousin and rise to these exalted heights herself. But each attempt she made would end in failure, and each failure would throw Terry back into the netherworld of Turdballness, where she would put on Maria Von Trapp dresses and romp around the house declaring that the "hills are alive." Thus refreshed, she would try again to grasp the brass ring of delinquency, and fail again, and the cycle would go on and on. But finally, she made the move that would send her postage-due into the land of the hopelessly bizarre. One night, armed to the gills with peach schnapps, Terry lost her virginity to Dominic. This occurred during one of Dom and Donna's perennial separations and at these times Dom always became—well, frisky. At any rate, the outcome of their encounter was a thoroughly silent, withdrawn Terry who one week later left town for St. Joseph's Immaculate Heart of the Virgin Mary, Mother of Christ convent in San Antonio, Texas. There she spent the rest of her formative youth teaching second graders how not to swear. Terry's "complexities" were buried in Bible classes, holy kick-ball and reruns of "Davey and Goliath" cartoons—until Tina's wedding day.

Terry was surprised that her pure little heart began pitter-pattering as soon as she boarded the bus for Tina's shindig. She was alarmed when it began thump-thumping as she entered the church. Mindful of her familial obligation to be the Holy Vitale, she contained herself. But somewhere between thinking about Dominic and actually seeing Dominic, her thump-thumping pure heart became full of holes and all her complexities started oozing out. She had a little drink. Her eyes became large. Her limbs became animate, quick, aching to touch, to hold, to flail every which way to the music. And then her heart spewed complexities all over the place as Dominic noticed her. Then talked to her. Then kissed her.

Now, she is Turdball become woman—and not one who would drink, make out and throw up in parking lots, but a full blown, mature mama dying to raise hell in a plush hotel suite—and Dom has the key. It's the bottom of the ninth. Terry's last stand. Will she break through? And if she does, will she only be hurled back, back, back, into Turdballness—or even beyond?

CONNIE MOCOGNI

The day that Connie's father skipped out, Mrs. Vitale dubbed her "poor." Poor Connie—nobody dresses her right for school. Poor Connie—nobody's there when she comes home in the afternoon. Poor Connie—having a TV dinner because her mother's out on a date. But the "poor" handle never made sense to Tina, Donna and Marina. "Connie dresses cooler than anybody! Connie has her own key to the house! She can watch anything she wants on TV and stay up almost all night! Poor? Connie has it made." And Connie would agree. Independent, tough, and smart, Connie's freedom made her the undisputed coolest of cool. At eleven, she already knew how to mix a screwdriver. By seventh grade she was dating high school boys. And at nineteen she married an older guy that nobody knew, and Connie became the first of her group to leave the past behind.

But a year later, Connie was back and more notorious than ever. Not only was she a divorcee, but she was soon living in sin with Barry (becoming the first in the group to have a real house with a real jacuzzi and a real dog). Then, she became pregnant and with characteristic irreverence refused to marry. Now in Tina's eyes Connie had gone from "cool" to "icon," and when it came time to choose her wedding party it was really no contest. Tina asked Connie to break the mold again by being perhaps the world's first eight-months pregnant maid of honor.

So Connie walks up the aisle in all her glory. She stands before the congregation with a fresh-cut bouquet in her hands and a Bible reading about lightheartedness tucked into her glove. Tina approaches the altar, Tony waits. The music plays; the wedding is on! And Connie feels ... old. There is something going on here—something very good and innocent and hopeful—and it makes Connie feel vaguely sad. Suddenly all her worldly experience, gathered so early, has placed her not up on a pedestal, but oddly apart. And for the first time, Tina has something that Connie wants—a loving, trusting Someone in her life. She will not marry Barry. Why? Because she's strong, or because it's a sure way to have power over him? Do her biting remarks and cynical humor make her a scrappy realist or just a girl afraid to hope? And is she rich with wisdom and independence? Or is she, after all, Poor Connie?

JOHNNY NUNZIO

"...Air conditioning! Refrigeration! Or, computer and copier technician! They called Acme, and they're glad they did. Call 1-800..." Johnny took down the number and almost simultaneously began to dial. "Don't be stuck in your old life anymore!" The phone picked up at Acme Technical School and Johnny touched his remote, rendering mute six toddlers singing the praises of disposable diapers. "Acme Technical, please hold." "I guess a lot of people are calling," Johnny thought. On the phone a shortened version of the T.V. ad played accompanied by "Get up and go!" music. Johnny's thoughts went into the future—his future as an air conditioning-refrigeration-computer-copier technician. He stands with "his own set of tools" next to a refrigerator and a hundred under-educated, Neo-Nazi dropouts in blue overalls all learning skills which will probably be proved useless in a glutted job market. The instructor singles him out. He looks like his dad, and sounds like him, too—drunk. "Wake up, kid! You lazy son-of-a-bitch...!" "Hello! Acme Tech!" Johnny stared at the T.V. Downstairs, Dad was yelling. "Son-of-a-bitch...!" Johnny hung up the phone. The pipes behind the bar must be plugged up again. Johnny heard his dad's footsteps heavy on the stairs as he flipped the sound on again and grabbed his pencil. "...Why be stuck in your old life? Call Stan's Academy of Fashion and join the exciting world of beauty technology, now! Call 1-800..." Johnny took down the number as his dad burst in the door. "John-John! Get your soft ass out of that chair and help me!" "Ok, Dad." Johnny shoved the number into his pocket as his dad disappeared down the steps back to the bar. "Lazy son-of-a-bitch!" said his dad. "...Why be stuck in your old life...?" said the T.V.

Johnny has grown up in the shadows: the shadow of responsible, tough, football-playing Prince Tony, and the shadow of his dad's firm belief that Johnny is a soft, sullen, worthless male version of his mother. Johnny thought at one time that Tony's marrying and leaving home would let some light in on him and give him the chance to show his dad that he has actually grown up into a pretty good guy. But as the wedding day approached, Dad started drinking more and the shadows actually became deeper and longer. Johnny came close a couple of times to doing things he'd never done before, like tell Dad that he is a hopeless old drunk and that Tony is not perfect. But instead he resolved to take the high road. He made a plan. He will follow Tony out of the Animal Kingdom, marry somebody great, and maybe return someday with a life that proves his virtues. "Hurry up, you lazy son-of-a-bitch! We gotta go!" Johnny looks into the mirror and hurries to tie his tie. He's already embarked on the first step of his plan. He's got the number. After the wedding he'll make the call to Stan's Academy of Fashion and get an apartment nearby. Then, he'll move out. He looks into the future. It's Tony's wedding day. Liberation day. It will be a good day to meet girls. A good day to dump the past. A good day to step out of the shadows.

MARINA GALINO

Marina has been devoted to Tina since kindergarten, almost as long as Tina has been devoted to trying to ditch her. In those days, Tina would express her love for Marina in subtle ways like asking her to get her coat out of the closet, then locking her in and running. But Marina never really got the message and over the years her persistent desire to be "in" with the gang paid off. She stuck it out through the constant teasing and being set up as the patsy. She persevered while being used for her car, her money and her exam answers. Finally, amidst all the dumping on and being left out, Marina found her place in the group. She is now and will ever be the gang's official Pain in the Ass.

Marina has learned that being "in" has its duties. Among these duties ... are to be at Tina and Donna's beck and call (particularly if they can't get a car for the night) and to shut up when asked. But being "in" has its benefits, too, and lucky for Marina one of them is the protection she receives, especially from Dom, against men who would cheerfully take advantage of her gullibility and talent for being kicked around and coming back for more. It's almost a full-time job because more than anything, Marina wants to be loved. As Dom would tell you, Marina brings out the sympathetic streak in anybody. So everyone helps out. Even Tina was once touched. In a spasm of pity back in the first grade, Tina asked Marina to be her bridesmaid.

About a week ago, Marina began to prepare for the big day. First, she began to cry. Then, through the tears, she got her gown, had her hair made over and collected things old, borrowed and blue. But then something happened that she hadn't prepared for. She got a date. And as she walks up the aisle today she can't help but marvel at the significance of the moment. Here she is—Tina's bridesmaid. How can you be more "in" than that? And to have a date! At a wedding! Her fortunes are truly changing! Through the tears, Marina sees her friends, the flowers, the candles on the altar. She sees Father Mark and Uncle Lui, Mrs. Vitale dressed in black; and she sees that her date— tall, handsome, beautiful, well-dressed Johnny Maritello— is nowhere to be seen. Marina's bubble bursts like Donna's gum but she never stops smiling. She dances and drinks and laughs with heroic gusto, see-sawing between attending to Tina, and hooking up with a man—any man— (preferably one attached to an expensive car and a Gold American Express Card). But even when she finds a guy, there is something missing. She finds herself drawn to the door, hoping that maybe her prince will come in. Sadly, the promise of this night died as she walked up the aisle and nothing can soften the hard truth. She has been dumped on again, just like always. And if she really wants love, she has got to change.

MICHAEL JUST

THUD THUD THUD THUD. Michael swerves, pulling the van back into his lane and off the reflectors. He looks at the speedometer and strains to bring the dancing numbers into focus. Sixty m.p.h. No problem. He grabs another malt liquor from the passenger seat—"her" seat—takes a swig and pulls into a break in the bushes onto a dirt road. As the van squeaks to a stop, dust sweeps past the window and into the trees. Dust. They call Michael "Dust." Polishing off his malt, Michael tosses the can into the back—warm sludge dripping onto the musty old futon. "This is the place ..." He sings the line from that old Lou Reed song and pops another brew. "This is the place where she ..." A silent wish sears his frame and comes to rest behind his eyes. If only it were last week, or last year. Cruising at night, heavy metal screaming, his long hair whipping out the window and that foxy teeny-bopper popping a beer for him. Tina. Shit. "I'm just tired of this, Michael." "Tired of what? Me? Tired of me?" "I don't know." Michael knows. He saw it coming. Never gonna get mixed up with a kid again. Tony Nunzio. Stupid jock. You'll get tired of him, too, the stupid jock!

Michael's voice sounds tinny and small, stuck in the van. He opens the window and sticks his head out. "You'll be back!" Better. A little echo. "You'll be back," he mutters, the demand punctuated by the crack of his last beer.

The reception hall is hot and the dancing has made his chest wet with sweat that smells like booze. Salt burns like hot forks on his skin. THUD THUD THUD. His heart bounces the bottle of Southern Comfort stuck in his waistband. The bottle and Michael's lips have been apart since re-hab and they've been kissing all evening in sweet reunion. Michael takes a long swig and laughs. When he walked into the church today a thousand shocked faces whirled on him. A thousand shocked faces and "her" face. He'd been gone a long time. Couldn't believe she was looking at him. She looked like she'd seen vomit. His chest itches like wildfire, scorching the earth, scorching his body. THUD THUD THUD. Someone runs by and Michael says "Hi" too late, they've long since gone. The music, the laughter, the shouts are a monolith of sound, a chorus that wails a crazy song of abandon. It rushes like rapids of fire into the demon's mouth where all is shadow and mirrors and heat and humiliation save a distant sliver of white that is Tina. Tina. His feet want to move and they move by themselves as a long wail joins the suffocating monster of sound pushing him, pushing him. The fire on his chest screams for release. His hair whips in the wind. He reaches the bandstand, heavy metal striking blows reaching deep into the sockets of his eyes. The demon opens his mouth again and emits a terrifying laughter of anguish set to music. Michael tugs at his shirt and buttons fly. He rubs his heart. The fire there turns into a triumphant stream of revenge that strikes Tina full in the face knocking her to the floor, dead. Michael flies away borne by unseen arms. He looks back one last time and sees Tina, now in a chair. He hits the ground hard. "Asshole." "Leave me alone!" His voice sounds tinny and small. Lying in the van, a little Comfort drips from Michael onto the musty old futon. "This is the place ..."

NUNZIO

Back in the old days, Nunzio was what they called a pipe guy. It was a simple job: find people who had crossed his bosses and administer one sharp blow to the offender's head with a pipe. It might be a wake-up call, or a down payment on treatment yet to come, but that wasn't his business. He was the pipe guy, nothing more. One day, out on a pipe mission, Nunzio was visited by one of those rare moments of clarity when a person gets a brief glimpse at the truth of his life and is offered a chance to change. Nunzio's partner, Big Harriet, had just pinned back the arms of an offender, exposing his head for piping. Suddenly, Nunzio was struck by the notion that his life was going nowhere. Hitting guys with a pipe. What was he getting out of it? He had his dreams, too, a world that he wanted to build. It wasn't getting built this way. He raised his pipe hand for the strike, and for the first time he saw the fear in his target's eyes. He hesitated, and the fear turned to...something else. "Whop him, Nunzio!" Harriet said. Nunzio saw the fear return. He hesitated again, and the eyes softened again. That was it! Nunzio's pipe hand dropped to his side. "How much do you owe?" he said. It was under a hundred. "Let him go. I'll pay it." Now Nunzio looked deep into the offender's eyes. Yep, that was it. This guy was grateful. "Come by later, we'll work something out." Nunzio turned and walked away, and he heard from behind: "Thanks, Nunzio." That was it. Somebody owed him something. He had planted his first hook. The cornerstone of his Kingdom had been laid.

"Find out what a guy needs and give it to him. Then he's on the hook. After that, you can collect however and whenever you want." Upon this principal, the Nunzio Kingdom has flourished. Now, in the graceful autumn of his reign, Nunzio sits in his basement room below the Animal Kingdom, listening to the gentle thud of music and the dancing feet of his strippers. He has an itch in his brain. The worm that lives there has been whispering darkly that somebody is wriggling off the hook. It's Tony. Prince Tony. He's getting married today, then he's gonna shack up with his girlfriend. Become a Vitale. Break up his Kingdom. Nunzio broods. The point of a royal marriage is annexation, not amputation. Nunzio pours a drink. Hooks. Hooks. He has to bring more than just a bottle of booze to this wedding, he's got to bring a couple of big hooks. First, the Scalia house, that great old Victorian the Scalias have been renting from him for years. As of today, it belongs to Tony. The second hook is for Tina's mom. It was planted long ago, but never reeled in. Tonight it will be. Josie Vitale. Why not? It would be nice to have a real woman around, especially for the girls upstairs. Nunzio pours another drink. Eleven a.m. The wedding's at three. Tired. Old. A whole life, casting, reeling, casting. Apartments, houses, mounds of cars, money. An empire, all got by hooks. But what good is it if it all falls apart when he's gone? Nunzio hears his voice: "Tony ain't my son no more." The worm won't shut up. He looks in the mirror. The eyes—what is that? "Fear," says the worm. Nunzio raises his pipe arm as if to strike. He hesitates, and the eyes become iron. "Meat-hooks, baby," says Nunzio. "Meat-hooks."

JOSIE VITALE

Josie believes that in life you should stick to what's real. Like shopping lists, and "Hawaii Five-0" at 10 p.m. Otherwise you just start dreaming, and dreams are a lightning rod for disappointment. Not that Josie hasn't had her share of dreams, but dreams lead to hope, and she has proof that hope is just a big practical joker. In a box in the spare room closet are all the photographs—Tina and Tony at the prom, Joey in his Senior Class play, and Vito—poor Vito—showing off the boat he was going to buy when he retired. The box is a testimony to hope, to plans. But where are the grandkids that were the promise of that prom night so long ago? Or Joey's first night on Broadway? Where is Vito? Struck down, like dreams always are. Better to stick to what's real. Like leaky faucets, and spoons in the garbage disposal. And photographs glimpsed in the dark on sleepless, airless nights.

Today is a big day for Josie, and she doesn't want any surprises. Behind Tina's wedding is a solid, verifiable battle plan backed by hard work, experience, and contracts in writing. The photographer has guaranteed three rolls of good stuff or she gets her money back. Same goes for the catering. Hand-rolled ziti with prosciutto. It's in the contract. The band will be on time and will play three hours with two breaks of fifteen minutes, and will be paid after the reception, last thing. Their money is already in an envelope in her purse. $500.00. And not a penny more. It's all in writing. And if there are any problems—well, there just better not be any problems. No surprises, period. Unfortunately, surprises have a way of surprising people, and there is one in store for Josie. The surprise is that life, no matter how hardened against hope, can be easily made hopeful by the slightest whisper of a dream. A dream can make a hard heart downright weak in the knees. And the sight of an old flame can transform a world-worn mother into a goofy teenage girl.

Josie has known Nunzio since high school. In those days, he was funny and exciting and his eyes sparkled as if he was always telling a dirty little secret. It's been a lot of years, but somehow he hasn't changed. That's the first surprise. The second surprise is that Josie hasn't changed all that much, either—she still likes it. With a couple of shots of vodka, a rose and a dance, she starts to feel as if a little window, long stuck shut, is sliding slightly open. A breeze sneaks in and it begins to whisper: she has been a mommy all her life, she's kept things together, she's made things perfect for everybody else. Maybe now—did his hand just brush her leg?—maybe now she ... needs ... something. Somewhere in the spare room closet there is a photograph of a young girl in a neatly pleated skirt standing next to a Chrysler convertible. A young man with sparkling eyes sits in the driver's seat tuning the radio to an old song—a good song, not like today. And as the blood trickles into the cheeks of that old photograph, a little dream begins to rise higher and higher like a lightning rod into the sky of Josie's life.

UNCLE LUI

A long time ago, Uncle Lui and his brother owned a bakery. It was in a nice building on a busy street with plenty of people who had plenty of money to buy goods from the Domenico boys—Guiseppi, the sly one, and Lui, the wise one. Customers found the bakery very handy because it was only steps away from a nice general store owned by another boy from the old country, Angelo Nunzio (Tony's grandpa). Now one day when the work was done, the Domenico boys and Nunzio were relaxing on the stoop when Nunzio suddenly had an idea. "Listen," he said. "Why donna we hava a little fire?" The Domenico boys didn't get it. It wasn't cold and there was nothing to barbecue. "No," Nunzio continued, "maka fire—inna the store! If we maka da fire inna the store we collecta de insurance and maka pile a money—the American way!" Well, Lui said "No!" and his brother said, "Shut up, Lui," and before the evening was out, it was all arranged. All that remained was to wait for the blaze, and the money. Nunzio was always one to try and keep business in the family and this job was no exception. The arsonists he enlisted were none other than his eight year old son Anthony and some of his pals who had been out clubbing rats all day and were probably tired, but that's no excuse. The fact is, when the smoke cleared, the bakery was destroyed and was so obviously a case of arson that the Domenico's were lucky not to have been brought up on charges. Nunzio's store, however, escaped with minor smoke damage. Nunzio took this outcome as proof positive that he never liked the Domenico brothers anyway and besides, "Hey, that's the waya it goes."

Thus, Uncle Lui was present at the birth of the ancient feud with the Nunzio family. Then as now, Uncle Lui is a true old-world gentleman. He is the patriarch of the family and the keeper of the family flame. The one with the most reason to hold a grudge, and the one least likely to do so. He lives by a principle that requires him to judge all people on their own merits, an outlook without which Tina would not be marrying Tony today. For Uncle Lui is the last word around in the Vitale family, and his blessing is sought in all matters of import.

Although he speaks only broken English, and can't get around very well any more, he has a power and a dignity that belies his frailty and the sad fact that he cannot survive without the aid of his niece Josie. As he presides over the marriage of his princess Tina, Uncle Lui sees all that goes on, and sees all that has gone before. He sees the father in the son, the daughter in the mother, the weakness and the pride, the foolish and the true and then he smiles inside and struggles out of his chair and slaps Tina across the face because she is acting like an imbecile. And then he has a little wine. Because he's Lui, the wise one.

GRANDMA NUNZIO

Back behind Nunzio's Animal Kingdom, nestled amongst the old cars and refrigerators, electrical conduit and concrete pipe, sits Grandma Nunzio's home. Built around 1951 and christened "The Travelmaster" it's a small trailer now set up on blocks and connected to the conveniences of modern life by a garden hose and a 100 ft. extension cord from Builder's Emporium. The flowers by the steps were planted there because that's where the hose leaked. She sits out by the old DeSoto because that's where a big scrap of carpet has always been. The tiny grave of Pancho the chihuahua is back by the right rear taillight because that's where he died. And she loves this place because Tony Nunzio's her son, and he told her that she's the Queen.

Although Grandma may be a woman unconcerned with and bewildered by the various found fabrics that have made up the quilt of her life, it is important to note that this quilt is stitched together with extraordinarily strong thread. Grandma has lived a mission—to have children, to see to it that they have children, and see to it that they, too, have children. And this mission burns as strongly today as it did when, as a young newlywed, she boarded a boat and sailed for America, toward the purpose of her life.

Today is a landmark day for Grandma. With the marriage of her grandson, she is seeing another cornerstone of her master plan laid into place. So she celebrates with a drinkie and talks of old times with Lui. She enjoys the food and stuffs her purse with leftovers for Pancho (she's a little forgetful). She even briefly cuts a rug with Joey. But don't be misled. This may be a send-off party for Tony, but it is also a kick-off party for her next and perhaps final battle—the quest to get Johnny married, too. Behind that wandering, mumbling exterior lurks the master architect of the Nunzio family tree. She draws a bead on every girl in the place. Each one is ripe, each one is marked, and each has the moral imperative to marry her last available progeny, or at least dance with him. There's no point resisting. After all, she's the Queen.

ROSE, JOSIE'S SISTER

Rose thinks that everybody should be happy, and in living this credo she has become a libertine, a freethinker, an uninhibited, straight-shooting, decidedly single woman of the people. She is the flip side of Josie in many ways, and if Josie knew all the ways, she would flip. For example, long ago when the young Mr. Nunzio would get fed up with Josie's "come hither—that's far enough" game, Rose was always waiting in the wings with a few games of her own. And nowadays when Joey is "too tired" to come home, (and happens to have a boyfriend in tow who's "too tired" too), Rose's heart, door and Jennifer Convertible is always open so the boys can "rest."

Yes, Rose is a real "Big City Gal," and in more ways than one. She's Big of heart, Big of size and Big with a certain something that men find irresistible. And she's City of mind and City of style with her posh little apartment and her job in a huge posh department store. It all adds up to a very cosmo lady who by virtue of a lifelong bubble-bath of restaurants, museums, dating and love-making has washed away all outward traces of her suburban upbringing and is not desirous of having them back.

But there are circumstances in which, regardless of the fine clothes one wears, or the mountains of hip magazines one reads, one is compelled to once again be the "mother" or the "daughter" or the "little sister" one would like to leave behind. Today is one of those days for Rose. Not that helping big sister Josie put this thing together hasn't been fun (truth be told, Josie couldn't have done it without her). But as the days have gone by and the old sister-to-sister relationship has begun to live again, Rose is beginning to feel less like the Mad Hatter of the City and more like Cinderella's Mop. She has to listen to Josie's worries and woes. She has to walk Uncle Lui around the hall and occasionally change his diaper. And she must not neglect her duties as the "cool aunt" who will cover for Joey when his boyfriend becomes indiscreet and for Tina when she gets too stoned. It all boils down to a lot of balls to juggle for one lady and the balls just keep on coming. Finally, she has to take the role of lady wrestler just to keep the people who want to kill each other from killing each other, and keep the people who don't want to kill each other from finding out what they should. And in the end she just wants to know—is everybody happy?

JOEY VITALE AND RICK DeMARCO

Alone in his bedroom, Joey wasn't listening to heavy metal bands, overheating with visions of pre-teen girls grabbing for his clothes. Nor was he reading Tom Swift or the Hardy Boys dreaming of inventions and sleuthing. No, Joey's room rocked with the sounds of "The Music Man," and when he danced before the mirror it was to a Broadway crowd. And when it came to reading, for Joey it was Dumbo—the story of the elephant who cried because his big ears made him the laughing stock of the whole circus. But Dumbo became a sensation when those silly ears made him able to fly. And whenever Joey felt blue because he couldn't live up to his father's expectations, or hurt as his mom tried to cut him from her apron strings, Joey would remember Dumbo and vow someday that he too would fly. He kept his vow. As soon as he entered high school, his ears started flapping. He discovered that he could sing and dance like nobody else, making him a celebrity on campus. He also discovered that he was gay, leading him to a secret life of weekend trips to the nearest town with a gay population. His reputation as an enigmatic artist grew and soon he even began to perform at community theaters—a feat unheard of for a student at Christ the King High. For those precious golden days, Christ The King High was Joey The King High—and it seemed it would never end.

But end it did, and like many big fish whose small pond has dried up, Joey was left to splash around in the mud puddle of past glories. His ears clipped, he now works as a bank teller and still lives at home—far from the bright lights of his Broadway dreams. Also like many whose hopes have run aground, the disappointment of it all comes out in a cynical humor that says: "I'm not like you, I'm really better than this. This is not my life." But this is his life, and thanks to Mrs. Vitale it's pretty comfortable. He still choreographs and directs community theater and the high school plays, and even though he has kept his lifestyle a secret from his mom, (this despite the fact his dad died doing the chores Joey abandoned for a notorious weekend) he has even found love—Rick DeMarco.

Today Rick is miffed because Joey would only let him come to the wedding "under cover" as the videographer. Although Joey explains that this way they can be together without people thinking they are "together," Rick sees it as a cowardly move. As the evening wears on, he begins to see Joey in a new light. Joey cracks snide remarks about people and makes faces behind his mom's back. He gets over-serious when one of his "works" is going to be danced by Tina and her bridesmaids. He even becomes embroiled in the ancient feud between the families he's supposed to be "better" than. Finally, in the harsh light of Rick's disgust, Joey too begins to see the chasm that exits between his "image" and the reality of his life. As he punches Johnny Nunzio, it all comes into focus—this wedding is like a pool-side beer party and Joey is stuck in the center deck chair. If he wants to fly again, he must start flapping now. Or Dumbo will cry evermore.

MADELINE MONROE

Maddy is Snow White in the enchanted cottage of Nunzio's Animal Kingdom. This fairy tale began when Nunzio noticed Maddy at a freeway coffee shop. Their eyes met, sparks flew, and within two weeks they were living together. Having found shelter from the storm that had been her life thus far, Maddy began working her magic. She and Grandma became fast friends watching the soaps, sewing costumes and baking weenies 'n' biscuits together. She became dream sister to Johnny, Tony and Dom and adoring lover to Nunzio—her Tony. And as a dancer she brought a breath of new life and luscious expertise to the Animal Kingdom that turned it into the most satisfying strip joint you could ever call home.

Today's page of the storybook sees Maddy excited, overjoyed and dewy with emotion because going to Tony's wedding is real proof that she has found a home at last. But any good fairy tale has to have a wicked witch and this one's name is Josie. Josie is adamantly against "one of Nunzio's floozies" attending the wedding. On hearing this, Maddy is crushed and doesn't want to go where she is not wanted. But Nunzio insists: "You're going. Number one, you deserve to be there. Number two, if you're good enough for me, you're good enough for anybody. And number three, stop being a baby. Besides, if you don't go then Old Pain ain't going because I'm not gonna watch her." And upon hearing her nickname, Grandma piped in: "You're going!"

So as Maddy helps Grandma up the aisle sporting a short shiny gold dress and a lot of cleavage, she is bombarded by disapproving stares from the Vitale family.

She feels shy and small and almost wants to just go back to the car. But as they continue, she begins to notice that many of the "faces" on Tony's side of the aisle are familiar, (although many of the ladies the "faces" are sitting next to aren't) and they are happy to see her. It begins to become clear that no matter who may disapprove, she is incapable of being anything other than herself. It also occurs to her that maybe "herself" is pretty good. And with that, she begins again to work her magic. Dancing, gabbing and turning the boys on, she fills the reception hall with that close, sexy, family feeling of the Animal Kingdom. At the end of the night she has proved to herself and anyone who is lucky enough to know her, that Maddy's heart is truly where the home is.

FATHER MARK

Father Mark thinks of himself as the "new breed" of priest, a short-sleeves-and-sandals kind of guy who really listens and really cares. Whether it's an off-color joke or a poem you wrote about your first sweetheart, Father Mark will listen—no judgements—and then he'll probably share a joke that he heard, or a poem he wrote. In the evening, you might find him sitting out in front of the church strumming a folk song on his guitar, singing in the baritone that he's very proud of. He's Andy Taylor with a mission.

Part of his mission has been to establish several progressive programs in the parish, designed to bring the community together and make the church a popular place. There is an after school athletic program (he referees all the games) and for the older folks there's bingo. All ages love the Las Vegas night complete with food from around the neighborhood and games of chance—roulette, wheel of fortune, craps. And then there's the monthly raffle which has really boosted Sunday attendance. He's also started a peer group—a place where the kids can "talk out what's bugging them" and maybe in the process receive a little bit of gentle guidance. It is here that he has gotten to know Tina and her friends, and where the kids have zeroed in on Father Mark's one weakness—he's a little bit of a pushover. And it's this weakness that turns what should be an easy wedding ceremony into a night of shame for Father Mark.

Father Mark is a little over-booked today. Rose Acupinte needs a visit in the hospital and he has to perform a sick mass that night as well. However, when he tells Mr.

Nunzio that he has to leave, he's met with a lot of resistance. Mr. Nunzio and Mrs. Vitale feel that, especially in light of their contributions to the church, (Mrs. Vitale is his top volunteer, Mr. Nunzio his top check-writer) he should—he must—stay. So Father Mark gives in, agreeing to stay until the food comes out. From this time on, every attempt he makes to sneak out is thwarted either by the parents' demands or the kids' genuine desire to have him around. It's in this spirit that Johnny convinces Father Mark to join him in a friendly shot of vodka, and here Father Mark's only other weakness is revealed. Before long, he has slid down the short slippery slope to all-out drunkenness. His journey through the land of booze unfolds in three stages. First, the Jack Benny in Father Mark emerges, as he entertains table after table with jokes and stories about his life and the lives of his flock. Next, the dark shadow of guilt falls as the image of Rose Acupinte lying alone in her hospital bed creeps into his loaded mind. Finally, his body hardly conditioned to large amounts of straight vodka, he succumbs to sickness himself. He ends up wandering the bar area crying. How can I be such a disgusting person? How will I ever face my parishioners? What must they think of me? If only he were able to see straight he would know—as this wedding winds down, he fits right in.

VINNIE & LORETTA BLACK
AND FAMILY

Vinnie Black is a man who has been waylaid en route to his destiny. Somewhere between one night stands as a fourth rate Catskill comic and hosting the Academy Awards, Vinnie acquired a wife, four kids, a lot of gold jewelry, a cheesy reception hall and became Vinnie Black the Cadillac of Caterers. Of course, Vinnie would tell you that this was his plan all along, and to watch him in action, you might even believe him. He moves through every event at the Coliseum like a sultan. His appetizers are exotic emeralds from the Far East and the pasta is a plate of gold with little ruby meatballs. And for dessert, the crown jewels—Vinnie's own stand-up monologue; material stolen from only the best. Yes, Vinnie is the king, the master of all he surveys. He's got it all, except one thing—the deed to the Coliseum. This his wife Loretta holds, and it's her hold on Vinnie.

Vinnie is not a family man. He's more of a horse man. And a Lotto man, and a poker man. If money can be laid on it, Vinnie will oblige. If it weren't for the infinite scope of Loretta's ability to find hiding places for their dough, the family would have nothing. Vinnie does have paternal instincts, although, they tend toward the totalitarian. He loves to have Loretta and the kids close to him—in the kitchen, over the dishes, on the stairs with a broom—and even in his comedy act. It is heartwarming to see his entire brood lined up behind him like a combination chorus-line/chain gang as he cracks his jokes. If Vinnie is the Cadillac, Loretta and the kids are the pick-up trucks.

This wedding will be distinctly grand because both Vinnie and Loretta have known the Nunzios and Vitales for years, and as with any group of peers there is peer pressure. Vinnie will be especially "on" today, to show Mr. Nunzio and Mrs. Vitale who really "made it" after high school. The children are under an unusual strain, too. Having to serve the food and clean up the messes of Tina and the "cool" crowd will no doubt seal their reputation as the town's only brother and sister team of "geeks." It is all too much for Mikey Black. After his performance as a wooden soldier in the "Champagne March" what little dignity he has left is stripped, having been crowned the "Toast King" and forced to wear an apron tied around his head. His chance for redemption comes in the form of Barry. Michael needs a drink, and Mikey can get booze from behind his father's bar. "Coolness" is within his grasp and soon so is a bottle. Stealing from the Father of the Coliseum is a vile thing— certainly too vile to be kept secret—and the beans are spilled by Mikey's younger sister. Furious, in the privacy of the kitchen, Vinnie deals Mikey a punishment that spells the end of his rule. For Loretta, the line has been crossed. Punching her is one thing, but her kids—that's too much. Although she and the kids continue their work, a quiet palace coup has taken place, and nothing will ever be the same for Vinnie. Now the kids know: Mom owns the building.

SAL ANTONUCCI, THE PHOTOGRAPHER

Sal doesn't like photography, and he doesn't like weddings. He doesn't like people and he hates babies. He also doesn't like his brother, Al. But, he does like the horses, and consequently, he always needs money. That's why he doesn't like Al. One day, Sal won an entire photography business off a guy on a horse bet. Now, Sal would have sold the equipment and put the money down on the next Exacta, but Al objected. Sal owed Al a lot of money, and Al swore he would turn off the cash unless Sal got a job. So presto, Sal became a photographer. Now, to make sure he photographed something, Al began to send his clients from the hair salon Sal's way. Soon, Sal was finding himself at weddings and graduations instead of the two-dollar window.

Today Sal wishes three things: that he had some money; that he had a portable hot-line phone linked up to the track; and that Mrs. Vitale had a different hairdresser.

DONNY DULCE AND FUSION

Donny is the heart throb of the local clubs—Sparks, Rumplestilskins, The Watering Hole. He knows he's every girl's dream, but what he doesn't know is that he's in the dreams of their boyfriends, too. They dream of punching his face in. However, the boys can't deny one thing—when Donny and his band play, the girls get worked up, and when that happens, the boys benefit. And, hey, nobody's girlfriend has ever whimpered "Donny" at the crucial moment. Not yet, at least.

TIMELINE

PRE-CEREMONY ONE:
THE BOYS ARRIVE

1. Sister Albert Maria places "religious folk song" lyric sheets on the pews as the guests begin to arrive. She is glowing—she is God's representative today and these are "His" lyric sheets.

2. Sal, the photographer, arrives. He has the races on his mind. He looks as if he's overslept and is only here by the grace of lots of sugar donuts. He surveys the scene and begins to set up.

3. Music blares from outside. A car pulls up and almost before it stops, four men pour out. They are in great spirits—almost high. It's their day and they rule. It is Tony, Johnny, Dom and Barry.

4. Dom immediately spots someone he can't help but put in a headlock. Johnny greets the first person he sees, flashing a smile (he is aware his dream girl may be watching). Barry hangs with Tony. He is Tony's right-hand man today, and he takes the position seriously. Tony melts into the scene like everybody's favorite flavor ice cream. His nervousness is balanced by his confidence and natural charm. Far from being edgy, he puts everyone else at ease.

5. CHURCH MUSIC BEGINS. (approx. time: 15 minutes for audience of 250 people)

6. Dom and Johnny begin to seat people on the "groom's side" or the "bride's side." Johnny seats people with an air of easy dignity, trying to shed his "little brother" image. After all, he is only moments away from being the eldest available Nunzio under fifty. Being seated by Dom, however, is a little like going through a car wash with no water. By the time one is seated he is likely to

have been frisked, kissed, or at least Italian face-slapped or pinched.

7. Sal rounds up Tony and Barry to have their picture taken. They are wound up and don't want to stand still.

8. While taking the pictures, Father Mark comes over to Tony and Barry, and tries to act like one of the guys. He offers his usual groom advice—"The back door's unlocked just in case you need it."

PRE-CEREMONY TWO:
THE FAMILIES ARRIVE

1. Tony looks toward the door and feels that familiar twist in his stomach—his dad has arrived. Nunzio is accompanied by his mother and his girlfriend, Madeline. As they work their way toward Johnny and Dom, Nunzio greets those he knows—which is everyone. He is very proud of Maddy and very annoyed that Grandma had to come. She has become Maddy's responsibility. Nunzio carries a plastic bag—he has brought his own bottle of Absolut. Tony takes a deep breath as he goes to greet his dad.

2. Nunzio calls to Johnny: "Get over here and get your grandma!" Johnny is the little brother again.

3. Johnny takes Grandma and they all make their way to the Nunzio pew. Nunzio and Maddy lag behind, Nunzio shaking hands and kissing ladies. It's his day and he feels like John Kennedy.

4. Maddy is seated with Grandma, and Sal calls Nunzio over to get a picture with Barry and Tony. Nunzio joins

them at the front of the church on the Vitale side. Nunzio insists that Maddy get in the picture too, and they all enjoy the view as she bounces over. Nunzio and Tony position Maddy between them and Nunzio raises her hem slightly. None of this is lost on Sister.

5. The Vitale Family arrives. Rose brings Uncle Lui up to the Vitale pew. Mrs.' Vitale stays in the back with Joey checking things out. Rick DeMarco enters and sets up his video equipment.

6. When pictures are over, Tony, Barry and Nunzio greet Rose and Lui. It is almost time.

7. Sister quiets the crowd, as the church music ends. In her best "Julie Andrews," she teaches them the "religious folk song" for the ceremony.

8. Hidden from view, Tina and her bridesmaids have their picture taken by Sal before the big moment. The girls give Sal a hard time because they enjoy ruffling his feathers.

PRE-CEREMONY THREE:
THE PROCESSIONAL

1. As "Ave Maria" begins, Joey escorts Mrs. Vitale up the aisle. She walks as though she has a crown on her head. It's *her* day. Joey is a little stiff. Nunzio remarks to Tony that Mrs. Vitale "used to be a goer." Tony is distracted now.

2. Mrs. Vitale greets her family. She is thrilled to see Sister Albert Maria, her niece. They share a warm embrace. They haven't seen each other in a long time. She goes to

the Nunzio side of the church where the devotional candles are and kneels in solemn ceremony to light one for her dead husband, Vito. She's doing her best today without him. Tony ventures over to say hello, and Mrs. Vitale shoos him away. Tony feels awkward and embarrassed by her brush off.

3. Tony gives her some space and then helps Mrs. Vitale to her feet. She straightens his tie. As she returns to her pew, she shoots Madeline a look of disdain.

4. Father Mark takes his place at the altar, and Nunzio sits between Maddy and Grandma. Tony and Barry stand in place.

5. "HERE COMES THE BRIDE" BEGINS (approx. time: 2 minutes)

6. Dom sees Donna for the first time in her bridesmaid outfit. They get horny and share a wet kiss. Johnny walks Marina up the aisle. This is not the girl he had in mind. Marina cries a lot. Her childhood friend is getting married and she has PMS.

7. Dom walks Donna up. Donna is forcing a "picture smile" and snapping gum. Mrs. Vitale motions for Donna to "give me the gum." Aggravated, Donna obliges.

8. Connie, the maid of honor and seven months pregnant, walks up alone. Mrs. Vitale cautions the video guy to shoot Connie from her chest up. Connie is nonplussed by the whole situation.

9. Tina is escorted by Joey. He loves his sister and really feels like the "man of the house." Tina is nervous and in shock. It feels like a dream. Despite her nerves, she is aware that this is "the most photographed day of her life." She wears a "picture smile," too. She can't believe how much she's shaking. She misses her dad.

10. As each member reaches the altar, they take their place in front of their chair. Tina, about to kneel, suddenly runs over to kiss her favorite, Uncle Lui. The bridal party and congregation remain standing as Tony and Tina kneel before Father Mark. The ceremony begins.

THE CEREMONY

(SAL arranges Tina's gown and positions himself in the aisle between the families. HE snaps some pictures as RICK takes a spot to the left of the Vitale pew to videotape.)

FATHER MARK. (*Blessing Tony and Tina.*) Oh, Heavenly Father, we are gathered here today to celebrate the banquet of life that God has given us and to witness the feast of love which Valentina and Anthony are to share in marriage. Let us begin by remembering that love must be a part of our lives and that we have not loved enough. Amen. Please be seated.

(TONY is the picture of cool. TINA gets stage fright as SHE looks out upon the congregation.)

FATHER MARK. (*To all.*) Hi.

(There is no response.)

FATHER MARK. Hello?
CONGREGATION. Hello, Father.

FATHER MARK. Welcome to God's house. Tony,
Tina ... relax. Make yourselves comfortable. Make
yourselves at home. Because after all, you are at home.
God's house is your house. (*To the congregation.*) And
your house. And your house. And your house. Isn't it?
(*Beat.*) Isn't it?

CONGREGATION. Yes, Father.

FATHER MARK. (*Walks down the aisle.*) But wait a
minute. I know what you're thinking, you're thinking:
"Father Mark, I'm not the Church." This building is the
Church, with its beautiful architecture and stained glass and
the big organ. And you come here once a week—or maybe
once a year. (*HE pauses, then turns à la Phil Donahue.*) Or
maybe, just maybe, you are the Church. Don't you see?
Look at everyone. Look at each other. Hi, Sally. Hi, Bob.
I've got news for you. And the news is, you are the
Church. (*Turning on Dominic.*) Dominic! You are the
Church.

DOMINIC. (*Embarrassed.*) Thank you, Father.

GRANDMA NUNZIO. (*Loud.*) I'ma the Church!

FATHER MARK. Bless your heart, Grandma Nunzio.
You are the Church.

(*MICHAEL enters from the back and awkwardly looks for
a seat.*)

FATHER MARK. (*Noticing Michael.*) Michael. It's
good to see you. (*To the congregation.*) Let's find Michael
a seat.

(MICHAEL sits down. The BRIDAL PARTY and the FAMILIES are visibly effected by his presence, especially TONY and TINA. He shouldn't be here.)

FATHER MARK. Michael! Do you know why it's so important that you've come here today?

MICHAEL. Yeah.

FATHER MARK. Why?

MICHAEL. *(Thinks for a moment.)* I don't know.

FATHER MARK. Because Michael, you are the Church. Let us pray. *(FATHER MARK heads for the altar.)* The responsorial psalm is ... *(Sings.)* Hear, oh Lord, the sound of my call.

(TINA prompts Michael to take off his bandanna. HE does.)

CONGREGATION. *(Sings.)* Hear, oh Lord, the sound of my call.

FATHER MARK. *(Reading from prayer book.)* "We pray for those who have lost their way. The hungry, the homeless, the destitute, that they may someday find their way back home—back to our house. We pray."

CONGREGATION. *(Sings.)* Hear, oh Lord, the sound of my call.

FATHER MARK. "We pray for those who are dearly departed, especially Vi Nunzio, Tony's mother, and Tina's father, Vittorio Vitale."

(MRS. VITALE gasps with emotion. TINA gets a little teary.)

FATHER MARK. (*To Mrs. Vitale.*) But we don't cry, Josephine. We don't cry because we know they now enjoy eternal rest with our Lord Jesus. Jesus Christ.

MRS. VITALE. Thank you, Father.

FATHER MARK. (*To the congregation.*) We pray.

CONGREGATION. (*Sings.*) Hear, oh Lord, the sound of my call.

FATHER MARK. We pray that you smile down upon us and give us your blessing in our efforts to maintain our parish, (Name of church), in particular Sister Brian's Bingo night and the CYO's annual "Just Say No to Drug-A-Thon." This year's jackpot is a color TV and VCR, and you can see Phil Mendotto about tickets. We pray.

CONGREGATION. (*Sings.*) Hear, oh Lord, the sound of my call. Hear, oh Lord, and have mercy.

FATHER MARK. You know, I'm not going to do all the talking here tonight. You are. Why?

JOHNNY. (*Aside to Dominic.*) 'Cause we're the Church.

(*DOMINIC gives Johnny a high-five. FATHER MARK is not pleased.*)

FATHER MARK. (*Sarcastic.*) Thank you, Johnny. Now we have two readings. Our first is from Corinthians and we'll hear from the bride's brother, Joseph Vitale. Joey?

(*JOEY jogs to the pulpit, kissing Tina en route.*)

JOEY. (*Reading.*) "Love is patient and kind. Love is not jealous or boastful. It is not arrogant or rude. Love does not insist on it's own way. It is not irritable or resentful. It does not rejoice in wrong but rejoices in the right. Love bears all things, believes all things, hopes all things, endures all things. When I was a child I spoke like a child. I thought like a child. I reasoned like a child. When I became a man—

(JOEY starts to laugh and TINA joins in. FATHER MARK gives them a disapproving stare as TONY rolls his eyes.)

JOEY. —I gave up my childish ways. For now we see in a mirror dimly but someday we'll see face to face. Now I know in part, then I shall understand fully even as I have been fully understood. So faith, hope, love—abide these three. But the greatest of these is love."

(JOEY returns to his seat. UNCLE LUI quietly scolds him.)

FATHER MARK. Thank you, Joey. Our second reading is from Ecclesiastes and we'll hear from the maid of honor, Constance Mocogni. Constance? Constance?

CONNIE. *(Correcting him.)* It's Connie. *(SHE saunters to the pulpit, unfolding a piece of paper. Reading.)* "A good wife makes a happy husband. She doubles the length of his life. A staunch wife is her husband's joy. He will live out his days in peace. A good wife means a good life. She is one of the Lord's gifts to those who fear Him. Rich or poor, they are light-hearted and always have a smile on their faces. A wife's charm is the delight of her husband and her womanly skill puts flesh on his bone—

(CONNIE and the rest of the BRIDAL PARTY laugh at the sexual innuendo. FATHER MARK darkens with anger and embarrassment.)

CONNIE. *(Correcting herself.)* —bones. A silent wife is a gift from the Lord. Her restraint is more than money can buy. A modest wife has charm upon charm. No scales can weigh the worth of her chastity. As beautiful as the sunrise in the Lord's heaven is a good wife in a well ordered home." *(SHE returns to her seat.)*

FATHER MARK. Thank you, Connie. It's good to hear the word of the Lord from your mouths my friends. I'm in a terrific mood today and you might think, "Well, it's a wedding. Priests love to do weddings." But to be honest, I've done my share of weddings. No, today's wedding is special because I have a special friendship with our bride, Tina. And I hope I can say with her entire family.

TINA. Yeah.

FATHER MARK. In Joey's reading, he said "love is patient" and we certainly exercised our patience today waiting for the flowers to arrive. But what struck me was when he said "love endures." Think about that. Love endures. Like wanting to say "I'm right" but saying "I'm sorry." Love endures. Or like Tina bringing the Camaro home—on the back of a tow truck. Love endures. Or like Tina spending hours cooking a beautiful dinner only to have Tony call and say: "Hon, I'm going out with the boys for a few beers. I'll be a little late." Love endures. But it's not just about Tony and Tina's love for each other. It's about God's love for them, and it's about your love and support for them, through the good times and the bad. Because I promise you there will be bad times.

(TINA makes a face: "what a jerk.")

FATHER MARK. But love endures. Love endures. And I love you, Tina.

TINA. (*Saccharin.*) I love you, too. Father.

FATHER MARK. (*Turns to TONY who is caught off-guard.*) And Tony, it seems incredible that you and I just recently got to know each other during pre-cana. Because I can honestly say in that short time—what, six weeks?—you and I have become great, good friends. And I love you, Tony.

TONY. (*Embarrassed.*) Whoa!

(The GUYS crack up.)

FATHER MARK. And I think tonight I can truly say we're all *la famiglia.*

GRANDMA NUNZIO. *La famiglia!*

FATHER MARK. That's right, Grandma Nunzio. And now it's time to light the ceremonial candles. The lighting of the separate candles represents their individuality and the lighting of the center, or unity, candle represents them coming together as one in marriage. Barry?

(BARRY gets his guitar and takes his place at the altar. FATHER MARK joins him to sing a hip church ballad. TONY and TINA each light a candle and use them to light the center candle together. THEY replace

*their candles and join hands on the altar. BARRY
continues to play under the following.)*

FATHER MARK. (*To the congregation.*) May the
peace of the Lord be with you.
CONGREGATION. And also with you.
FATHER MARK. May our families exchange the sign
of peace.

*(MRS. VITALE and NUNZIO meet in the center aisle. HE
kisses her on the cheek and gives her a little "love pat"
on the butt. TONY and TINA exchange the sign of
peace with EACH MEMBER of the two families.
THEY return to the altar.)*

FATHER MARK. Now, Tony and Tina have prepared
two special readings to express their love for each other on
this, their wedding day. Tina?

*(TINA and TONY go through a "You go first," "No, you
go.")*

FATHER MARK. (*Insisting.*) Tina.

(BARRY switches to a classic rock melody.)

TINA. "*Love Grows*" by Tina Vitale. Love grows, like
flowers in the spring. Love grows, it makes me want to
sing. Give it kindness. Handle with care. And before you
know it—you're in love, you're a pair."

(SHE forgets her lines. JOEY prompts her audibly.)

TINA. "Love grows in twinkling stars, in holding hands, and kissing in cars. God's the gardener in this field of love. We're the seedlings that HE waters from above. With the sunlight of friendship nurturing our life, we bloom together as husband and wife."

(TINA playfully sticks her tongue out at Joey as SHE returns to her seat. TONY stands and takes a piece of paper out of his pocket. BARRY switches rock melodies.)

TONY. *(Inaudibly.)* "Love merges the lesser and the greater. Love merges me with the universe. My quest in life, is that of love—"
GRANDMA NUZIO. Tony, speak up. I can't hear you.

(TINA encourages Tony to continue.)

TONY. "—love is the eye of the universe—"
RICK. Tony, could you speak up? I'm not getting you on the audio.

(BARRY stops playing.)

TINA. *(To Rick, concerned.)* Did you get mine?
RICK. Yeah.
FATHER MARK. *(Sotto.)* Tony, just read a little louder.

(TONY is visibly miffed. BARRY resumes playing.)

TONY. (*Very loud and fast.*) "Love merges the lesser with the greater. Love merges me with the universe. My quest in life is that of love. Love is the eye of the universe. The window to the soul. The heart of my heart. This truth is my existence, the cosmic absolute. We are all connected, myself, my father and you.

(*HE acknowledges his dad. NUNZIO, delighted, waves to him.*)

TONY. "Love is time without beginnng or end. How do you acquire love? (*To Tina, with authority.*) Just take it. (*Reading.*) Don't force it or fight it. Just live it. I am love, therefore, I am loved."

(*TONY sits down. TINA is touched.*)

FATHER MARK. And now let us all raise our voices in song to Yahweh as Tina's cousin, Sister Albert Maria, leads us in [name of 70's religious folk song].

(*SISTER ALBERT MARIA leads the congregation in a 70's religious folk song accompanied by BARRY. TINA isn't pleased that her turdball cousin is singing and SHE expresses this to her mother.*
During the song, JOEY mimics Sister and the GIRLS laugh. At the end of the song, SISTER thanks Father Mark and sits down.)

FATHER MARK. And now as Tony and Tina take their vows and become one, let us all become one. Will you all please join hands?

*(EVERYONE does so, but UNCLE LUI has to go to the
bathroom. HE gets up and goes down the aisle followed
by AUNT ROSE.)*

FATHER MARK. Tony, Tina. Do you come here
freely and of—
MRS. VITALE. *(Anxious; re: Uncle Lui.)* Father
Mark. Can you wait two minutes?
FATHER MARK. *(To Rick.)* Is the video running?
RICK. Yeah.
FATHER MARK. Then we'll continue.
MRS. VITALE. *(Protesting; to Tina.)* He's going to
miss everything!
FATHER MARK. Tony, Tina. Do you come here
freely and of your own accord?

(THEY indicate "yes.")

FATHER MARK. Tony, repeat after me: I, Anthony
Angelo.
TONY. I, Anthony Angelo.
FATHER MARK. Take you, Valentina Lynne, to be
my wife.
TONY. Take you, Valentina Lynne, to be my wife.
FATHER MARK. I promise to be true to you in good
times and in bad.
TONY. I promise to be true to you in good times and
in bad.
FATHER MARK. In sickness and in health. And
forsaking all others give only unto you.

TONY. In sickness and in health. And forsaking all others give only unto you.

FATHER MARK. I will love you and honor you all the days of my life, 'til death do us part.

TONY. I will love you and honor you all the days of my life, 'til death do us part.

FATHER MARK. Tina.

(TINA repeats the above vows.)

FATHER MARK. And now the rings.

(BARRY brings the rings to FATHER MARK, who blesses them.)

FATHER MARK. Tony, repeat after me: Take this ring as a sign of my love and my fidelity.

(TONY places the ring on Tina's finger.)

TONY. Take this ring as a sign of my love and my fidelity.

FATHER MARK. Tina?

TINA. (*Places the ring on Tony's finger.*) Take this ring as a sign of my love and my fidelity.

FATHER MARK. If anybody knows of any reason why these two should not be joined in holy matrimony, let them speak now or forever hold their peace.

(EVERYONE holds their breath anticipating a move from Michael. TONY and TINA fix a gaze on him.)

FATHER MARK. And now, by the power vested in me by the state of (name), I now pronounce you husband and wife. Go in peace to love and serve the Lord.

(TONY and TINA kiss.
The recessional plays as the NEWLYWEDS run down the aisle to the applause of the congregation. TONY and TINA kiss the bridal party and make their way to the receiving line, as UNCLE LUI returns from the bathroom upset that he's missed everything. TINA poses with him for a photo taken by SAL.)

THE RECEIVING LINE

1. The wedding party and family form two lines by the door, making an aisle for the guests to file through. All are greeted, hugged, kissed and especially complimented as they go through into the cocktail room.

2. Maddy comes back to the receiving line and stands behind Nunzio. She is feeling a little shy, not knowing many people. Nunzio brings her into the line next to him. Mrs. Vitale refuses to let her stay. She says, "it's just for family."

3. When nearly all the guests have gone through the line, Father Mark pulls Nunzio aside and tells him he has to go visit a mutual friend, Rose Acupinte, in the hospital. Nunzio raises a minor stink. Mrs. Vitale overhears and absolutely will not let Father Mark leave.

4. Michael has been hanging around, not sure if he should just go in or not. Mrs. Vitale, after a gentle

grilling, invites him to stay. Sister Albert Maria (Terry) says "hello" to Dominic. It's the first time she's seen him in over a year. She's very shy but seems glad to see him. Donna doesn't like the exchange at all and warns Dominic to stay away from her.

5. Inside the cocktail room, the wedding party assembles for a picture. Sal has his hands full rounding everyone up and getting them into position. The natives are restless—they want to party. Sal counts off: "One, two, three!" and the wedding party boys flip Sal the "bird." Another attempt at the picture is made, this time successful. The bridal party makes a bee-line for the reception hall. The guests and family members follow them.

IN THE RECEPTION HALL

1. On Mrs. Vitale's insistence, Tina and Connie go to the bridal suite to await the introduction of the wedding party.

2. BAND PLAYS SONGS #1 & 2: (Light jazz standards. Approx. time: 4 minutes.) Vinnie, Loretta, and the Black family seat the guests and serve appetizers. Donna grabs Dominic. They love to dance and show off their latest moves (i.e., the Lambada).

3. Michael finds Barry to help ease him into the reception hall. Even though Mrs. Vitale sort of invited him, he's nervous about Tony and Tina's reaction to him.

4. The Vitale and Nunzio families settle into their respective tables. Nunzio pours drinks at the table from his bottle of Absolut.

5. Mrs. Vitale finds a seat for Michael by approaching a table of "friends" and explaining that Michael is a late addition, but "he's not a bad kid. Just a little mixed up." She signals for Michael to come over and sit.

6. BAND PLAYS SONGS #3, 4 AND 5 (Upbeat pop standards. Approx. time: 6 minutes.) The families, wedding party and guests mingle and dance. Marina looks for her date. Joey and Rick have a clandestine meeting. Loretta helps Father Mark find his seat. Johnny dances with cute girls. Grandma Nunzio snoops around the buffet table.

7. Tony takes Michael aside and warns him not to get out of line. Barry assures Tony everything will be fine. Michael tells Tony he'll be cool.

INTRODUCTION OF THE
WEDDING PARTY

1. DONNY. Alright. If our beautiful guests could find a seat, we're gonna try to get this party off to a rolling start. The first thing I want to know is "How's everybody feeling tonight?" (*Not satisfied with the response.*) Let's try that again—"HOW'S EVERYBODY FEELING TONIGHT?!"

(*The CROWD cheers.*)

DONNY. That's better. My name is Donny Dolce and we—are—Fusion! We'll be in charge of all the musical happenings here this evening. What we're gonna do right now, folks, is bring those two kids in here that this whole wonderful evening is about. Now, when I call them, I want you all to clap and scream and make them feel very welcome. Because a day like this only comes once in a lifetime ... we hope! So, let's start by introducing some gorgeous people, the beautiful bridal party. Let's do it!

(A jazzy version of "Here Comes the Bride" plays. DONNY reads the following off index cards.)

DONNY. First, I want to introduce to you, the two people who made Tony and Tina possible ... the mother of the bride—the enchanting Mrs. Josephine Vitale and the dapper father of the groom, Mr. Anthony Angelo Nunzio, Sr.!

(THEY enter waving and, guided by LORETTA, take their place on the dance floor. NOTE: The remaining BRIDAL PARTY follows suit as their names are announced.)

DONNY. Right now, we're gonna call our first very beautiful bridesmaid, accompanied by the dashing brother of the groom Please welcome Miss Marina Galino and Mr. Johnny Nunzio. Next, let's say "hi" to another one of our stunning bridesmaids, accompanied by her handsome boyfriend—Miss Donna Marsala and Mr. Dominic Fabrizzi.

(DOM "high fives" MICHAEL en route to the dance floor and practically knocks him out of his seat.)

DONNY. Get ready to meet two very, very special people—this sexy lady is our maid of honor and this dude is our best man. Let's hear it for Connie Mocogni and Barry Wheeler!

(THEY enter like movie stars at a premiere.)

DONNY. That is one good lookin' bridal party! At this time, I want everybody on their feet. Come on. Stand up as I introduce to you for the first time, as man and wife— Ladies and gentlemen, Mr. and Mrs. Anthony Angelo Nunzio, Jr.

2. BAND STRIKES UP "2001: A SPACE ODYSSEY" ["Thus Sprach Zarathustra"] (Approx. time: 20 seconds.) The wedding party face their partners and raise their arms to form a canopy for Tony and Tina—the king and queen.

3. Tony and Tina enter and run beneath the canopy. Tony punches into the air at the hands that form the canopy. They run through once, come around, and go through again.

4. As Tony comes around, Barry and Dom start goof-fighting with him.

THE FIRST DANCE

1. THE BAND BEGINS SONG #6: (A romantic pop song Approx. time: 3 minutes and 20 seconds.)

DONNY. Bridal party, we need you to clear the floor so that Tony and Tina have plenty of room for their first dance as husband and wife.

(EVERYONE backs off as TONY and TINA have their first dance together. As THEY dance, MICHAEL tests the coolness of his table by professing to be on the wagon. HE says that being sober is no big deal. It's just an idea he's been checking out. AUNT ROSE comes by and starts asking specific questions about rehabilitation in a very loud voice. SHE offers to buy Michael a club soda.)

DONNY. Will the proud parents please join our newlyweds on the dance floor?

(MRS. VITALE and NUNZIO dance with their new children. TINA can't hide her disgust while dancing with Nunzio.)

DONNY. Bridal party, why don't you jump on in?

(THEY do so. And after a few moments:)

DONNY. Alright, it's time to grab a new partner because it's snowball time!

(The BRIDAL PARTY chooses new dance partners as EVERYBODY joins in. Only CONNIE and BARRY do not participate. THEY have become locked in a passionate kiss and are oblivious. The BRIDAL

PARTY forms a large "hugging circle" with the GUESTS, swaying and singing the last few lines of the song. BARRY and CONNIE are still kissing.)

DONNY. Let's hear it for Tony and Tina!

GRANDMA NUNZIO FALLS

1. DONNY. Okay, folks. The ceremony is over and we are here to do one thing! So come on, let's celebrate!

(BAND PLAYS SONG #7: Upbeat party song. Approx. time: 2 minutes and 30 seconds.
EVERYONE dances except CONNIE and BARRY who have yet to come up for air. DOM and DONNA are doing a very sexy dance. MICHAEL asks someone to dance. HE dances awkwardly and very energetically.)

DONNY. Ladies and gentlemen, I want to introduce my band. The man to my left, the ambassador of the bass, Mr. Carlo Cannoli!

(CARLO plays a short solo as does EACH MEMBER of the band upon their introduction.)

DONNY. The cat behind me is known as "the rock"— Folks, on drums, Mr. Rocco Caruso! And standing to my right, the sexy celestial—Miss Celeste Romano. And I am Donny Dulce. And what are we?!
ENTIRE BAND. WE ARE FUSION!

2. Joey gets the idea that it would be fun to dance with Grandma Nunzio. He takes her up out of her chair and brings her to the center of the dance floor. He begins to do a little "swing dance" with her. Grandma stays stationary. Giddy, Joey dances around her in a circle. Everyone is laughing. Somehow Grandma slips and falls. Joey is horrified.

3. Father Mark yells at the band to stop playing. Mrs. Vitale sees Grandma go down and screams: "Grandma Nunzio is dead!"

4. Connie and Barry continue their kiss. Tony, Johnny and Dom rush to Grandma as does Tina, Donna and Marina.

5. Tony announces: "She's not dead." Tina, seeing this is true, storms away mad because Grandma stopped the fun and stole attention from her. She decides to have a quick shot at the bar with Marina to calm herself down. Father Mark comes to Grandma. Vinnie calms the crowd.

VINNIE. Ladies and gentlemen, Grandma had a slight spill. She's going to be alright. And we're going back to Donny Dulce.

(The BOYS help GRANDMA to her seat. TINA assures everyone that Grandma is fine, she just wants attention.)

PICTURES FOR THE MANTLEPIECE

1. DONNY. We're gonna keep the party rolling with a medley of Tina's favorite songs.

(The band plays SONG #6, a medley of 3 dance hits. Approx. time: 5 minutes.)

2. Nunzio comes over and yells at Joey for allowing Grandma to fall. He then scolds Grandma for allowing herself to fall. He threatens to make her sit in the car. She cries a little. Father Mark is shocked, and Johnny tells his dad that he should go easier on her. Nunzio doesn't listen and takes Maddy back onto the dance floor. Father Mark and Johnny comfort Grandma.

3. Tina and the others dance. Tina thinks she's on MTV and performs for Rick and the video camera. Nunzio and Maddy dance for Grandma to cheer her up. Sal insists on pulling Tina out of the action for some posed shots on the dais.

4. Barry and Connie have lipstick all over their faces. Connie gets some napkins from the bar and wipes her kisses off Barry.

5. During first song of dance medley Sal takes a picture of Tony and Tina at the dais. This is the serious picture, the one you send to people who couldn't come. Tina dashes back to dance floor and continues dancing.

6. During second song of dance medley, Sal gathers the Vitale family at their table for a picture with Tony and Tina. All Tina wants to do is party. Sal is a real pain in her ass. But finally, she comes to the table and is

photographed. As soon as the flash goes off, she's right back out on the dance floor.

7. During third song of dance medley Sal gathers the Nunzio family at their table. Everyone is there except, of course, Tina. Sal pulls her off the dance floor. She sits. The picture is taken and she is out of there almost quicker than the flash of the camera. Nunzio insists that Sal get a picture with "all his boys" meaning Barry and Dom.

8. The medley ends. Tina, Marina and Donna want Donny to play more dance music. They were just getting warmed up. Tina rats on Donny to her mother with Donna. Mrs. Vitale, en route to reprimand, finds out that dinner is about to be served by Vinnie. She tells Tina to sit down. Tina mopes her way up to the dais with Donna. Donny asks everyone to take their seats.

THE CHAMPAGNE MARCH

1. DONNY. Right now, I want to introduce you to the gentleman who owns this fabulous room. He's going to be your host for the evening. Please welcome, Mr. Vinnie Black!

(VINNIE BLACK takes the mike and introduces himself and his family as if he were proclaiming peace on earth.)

VINNIE. Thank you, Donny. Thank you very much. I want to welcome all the Vitales and the Nunzios to this wonderful extravaganza. In case you didn't hear, my name is Vinnie Black and yes, I am the "Cadillac of Caterers." I'll be your host for this marvelous evening. Right now we're gonna do something I call my Champagne Ceremony. But, this is not your ordinary Champagne Toast. This is my "Fountain of Youth Celebration for Newlyweds." My friends, what you are about to see, I have not done since 1971 when my dear friend, Joey Heatherton [or name of a flashy local celebrity], got married right here in this very room. Today, I do it again for Tony and Tina. The Champagne March! (*Takes his place at the head of the march.*) DIM THE LIGHTS!

3. THE BAND PLAYS "MARCH OF THE WOODEN SOLDIERS" as the Black family, led by Vinnie, do the "Champagne March." This march is a tacky tradition at the Coliseum. The staff holds cheap sparklers as Vinnie holds aloft a broadsword. When the march is over, he and Loretta pour champagne for the bride and groom. All are duly impressed.

THE TOASTS

DONNY. All right, ladies and gentlemen. There's a special guy here tonight and the reason he's special is ... he's Tony and Tina's best man—Mr. Barry Wheeler!

(*DOM gets EVERYONE to chant: "Barry! Barry!" as Barry takes the floor like a Roman conqueror.*)

BARRY. Let's have a big hand for Donny Dulce and Fusion. A very righteous band from—[Name of a local bogus area]. They'll be puttin' on the hits all night. Right now, it'd be my pleasure if you'd join me in toasting Tony and Tina by picking up your champagne glasses or whatever you're drinkin' and helping us get this marriage off on the right foot. (*Turns to Tony and Tina.*) Tony and Tina, it's an honor for me to be your best man. Last night, Connie and me were lyin' in bed ... talkin' ... And somethin' popped out of my mouth. And I wanna repeat it right now. "I'm not only gonna be your best man for your wedding day, Tony and Tina. I'm gonna be the best man for the rest of your lives."

TONY. That, uh, blew me away, Barry. I'd like to make a toast right now to the most important person in my life ... my beautiful wife, Tina. She's put up with me for a few years already and I hope to God she puts up with me for the rest of my life.

TINA. I wanna make a toast, too.

MRS. VITALE. (*To the Vitale table.*) Tina's makin' a toast, now.

TINA. Paula Abdul, "FOREVER YOUR GIRL" [or current pop artist and hit] is my favorite video and I swear to God, Tone, I'm forever your girl.

(*This should be the end of it, but NUNZIO has decided that he'd like to make a toast, too. HE takes the mike from Barry.*)

NUNZIO. Everybody else is sayin' somethin'. I wanna say somethin', too, shit. Tony and Tina ...

(TONY and TINA are kissing.)

NUNZIO. Hey, put it down, boy. You got the rest of your life for that crap. It don't get no better, neither. Believe me. I just wanna say, Tina, I love you. You're a beautiful girl and you're my daughter now ...

(If he's making a toast, then I'm making one, too is MRS. VITALE's attitude as SHE cuts off the rambling Nunzio.)

MRS. VITALE. We wanna make a toast, too!

MR. NUNZIO. Right on. Here's your mommy. *(HE hands her the microphone.)*

MRS. VITALE. Thank you, Mr. Nunzio. Tony and Tina ... On behalf of the Vitales ... On behalf of the Domenicos ... And on behalf of my late husband, my Vito ... *(SHE breaks down, sobbing.)*

(MICHAEL has added all this up and decided that it must be "open mike." HE steps up to show his goodwill towards Tony and Tina.)

MICHAEL. I'd like to make the next toast. Tony and Tina ... wherever you go, there you are.

(The Vitales feel that Uncle Lui, as patriarch, should have the last word.)

UNCLE LUI. I wanna make a toast.

BARRY. Tony and Tina, Uncle Lui wants to say something.

UNCLE LUI. Tina, Tony ... *Figli maschi. Tanti Aguria a tutti.*

EVERYBODY. *Agurri!*

(BARRY takes possession of the mike again and asks everyone to give a big cheer for Tony and Tina. EVERYONE does. Happy to finally get to drink, CONNIE starts to down her champagne. TINA stops her and gives her hell for drinking while pregnant.)

THE PAPAL BLESSING

JOEY. (*Taking mike from Barry.*) Could we have a big hand for Barry Wheeler?! (*Applause.*) Okay! My name is Joey Vitale and I have two things to say. The first of which is you can sit back down and while you're getting comfortable, I'd like to get my sister down here because we have a surprise for her. And please bring down my fabulous new brother-in-law, Mr. Anthony-Oh-my-God-could-you-die Nunzio.

TINA. (*Approaching the dance floor.*) What are you doing?

JOEY. It's a little surprise from my cousin, Terry and myself. It's all the way from Rome—It's nothing big. It's nothing special. Oh, perhaps it's just a papal blessing from the Pope! That's all!

TINA. (*Thrilled.*) Oh my God! I love the Pope!

(SHE kisses Joey, Terry and the blessing. SHE shows it to the crowd.)

TINA. Tony, look at this! Isn't it gorgeous? Sal, get a picture!

(SAL does so.)

TONY. Joey, Terry, thanks. Excellent picture of the Pope. But, we got a problem here. The Pope spelled my name wrong.

TINA. (*Seeing the awful truth.*) Terry! It says "Antinio"!

TERRY. It's still holy!

TONY. (*Heading back to the dais.*) See what happens when you get a Polish pope?

TINA. Tony! Don't make fun of the Pope. It's not funny!

TONY. Tina, I think the Pope has a sense of humor.

TINA. It's a sin!!!

THE BLESSING OF THE FOOD

(As VINNIE introduces Father Mark, MADDY takes the papal blessing and shows it to Grandma. GRANDMA kisses it and MADDY tells her not to get spit all over it. JOEY takes it back, not hiding his disgust.)

VINNIE. OK, ladies and gentlemen. Right now, I want to re-introduce a very wonderful man who's going to do the blessing of the food.

(FATHER MARK comes forward and calms everyone down. HE gives his prayer.)

FATHER MARK. Thank you. As we say a little prayer before we eat at this wonderful occasion for our lovely Valentina and our handsome Anthony, I ask that we all bow our heads. In the name of the Father, the Son, and the Holy Spirit... Oh heavenly Father, we ask that you bestow your blessings on our Valentina and Anthony and may they be blessed with a healthy, happy and long life together with many children. And may I ask for all those gathered here who travelled far and near, may they have a safe journey home. In the name of the Father, the Son, and the Holy Spirit. Amen. And now ... *mangia.*

INTRODUCTION OF THE FOOD

VINNIE. Thank you very much, Father Mark. A wonderful man with a wonderful mission. Ladies and gentlemen, before I open up my fabulous buffet of love, I just want to tell you a little bit about it. In my food, I use all the ingredients Josephine's mother's mother's mother used. I use thyme, I use oregano, I use fresh basa de gol. But the most important spice I put in my food, my friends, is what we have in this room here tonight and do you know what that spice is called? (*Pause as HE waits for everybody to respond*.) LOVE! You got it. A pinch of love. And Tony and Tina?—I don't stop at the love. I get all my ingredients—all natural, all orgasmically grown, nothing artificial goes into my food. The salad you're gonna experience tonight—is the Vinnie Black Honeymoon Salad. Because it's just "Lettuce Alone Tonight." That's right! So, ladies and gentlemen, get ready for my GRAND BUFFET. Roll it out, please!

(The music from "2001: A Space Odyssey" plays. The food comes out.)

VINNIE. And ladies and gentlemen, to tell you how we're going to do this is my lovely wife, Loretta!

LORETTA. Thank you, Vinnie. Alright! This is what we're gonna do now. We're gonna form two lines—one on the right side of the buffet table—the other on the left side. Starting with the bridal party up there, followed by the two families—Josie and her wonderful family over here and Tony Nunzio and his family over there—followed by tables 1 through 10, and please wait 'til they are served. And then, followed by all you other people. You got that? Good. Let's eat!

DINNER ONE—"NO PROSCIUTTO IN THE ZITI"/BREAD FIGHT

DONNY. On behalf of Donny Dulce and Fusion, we wish you all a delicious "bon appetit!" And we'd like to offer a little music for your dining pleasure.

(BAND STRIKES UP SONG #8, an upbeat top 10 hit. Approx. time: 1 minute and 45 seconds.)

1. The wedding party and guests line up for food as per Loretta's instruction. Tina insists on going first and scolds Marina who tries to cut in front of her. Nunzio yells to Johnny, "Get down here and get a plate for your grandma." Maddy gets Nunzio a plate. Barry gets a plate for Connie. Father Mark comes by Nunzio's table to say he's leaving. Nunzio berates him into staying. Mrs. Vitale moves Michael to the front of the line explaining that he's practically family.

2. BAND PLAYS SONG #9 (A fun "Italian" song. Approx. Time: 2 minutes and 15 seconds.) As Tina gets back to the dais, she looks at her plate in horror. She yells across the hall, "Mommy! Mommy! There's no prosciutto in the ziti!" She tears down to her mother. Mrs. Vitale is shocked, they paid for it. She won't be taken advantage of because she is a widow. They call Vinnie over and confront him near the buffet table. Vinnie agrees to lower the price. Tina asks Uncle Lui if she can have the money. He says "yes."

3. Tina returns to the dais to tell Tony the good news and gets a bowl of pitted black olives which she sticks on her fingers and offers to her guests promising that they will "make you horny." Tina notices Father Mark without food. She brings him to the front of the line, explaining, "He's a priest. He doesn't have to wait." Nunzio sends Maddy to the dais to tell Johnny and Tony that he wants them to eat with him. They'd rather not.

4. BAND BEGINS SONG #10 (A medium "soft rock." Approx. time: 2 minutes.)

5. Nunzio decides to throw bits of bread at Johnny and Tony at the dais. The boys think this is great and retaliate with a food fight. Tina complains to her mom and Mrs.

Vitale approaches the dais to stop them. Nunzio puts bread in Josie's hair when her back is turned.

6. Mrs. Vitale returns to her table. Nunzio joins her and regales all with exaggerated tales of the bawdy times he and Mrs. Vitale had when they were in high school. Terry tries to strike up a conversation with Dominic. Donna basically tells her to get lost.

7. Michael approaches Barry and asks him to get him a beer. Barry gives in and they begin to make their way to the bathroom.

NOTE: A fourth dinner song can be added if there is a large audience.

DINNER TWO—PICTURES AT THE TABLES

1. DONNY. We're gonna take a short break after this instrumental. Enjoy your dinner. We're gonna do the same and we'll see you soon.

2. Sal gets Tony and Tina and takes them around to each table for a photograph. This is a chore for Tony and Tina, but to make it fun they torture Sal. On the count of three, instead of saying "cheese," they say "dick"!

3. Marina looks for her date, Johnny Maritello. She fears he's standing her up, but she won't admit it.

4. Nunzio has watched Celeste move to the bar with great interest. He goes there, too, and works his magic on her.

5. Barry has rounded up some guests to go to the bathroom to smoke pot. Michael comes in. Barry gives him a beer, which he chugs down.

6. Tina and Sister steal a moment to sneak a cigarette together, just like when they were kids.

7. Donna approaches Donny about singing with his band. She is being pretty flirty. Dom comes over and threatens Donny.

8. At the bar, Maddy has overheard the juiciest part of Nunzio's "come-on" to Celeste. Celeste and Maddy fight. Nunzio takes Maddy outside to cool her down.

AFTER DINNER: TINA AND MICHAEL DANCE TO "THEIR" SONG

1. The Band takes the stage. BAND STRIKES UP SONG #11 (Funky up-tempo. Approx. time: 2 minutes.)

2. Donna can't take anymore of Dominic's petty jealousies. He can't stand her flirting. They fight and decide to break up.

3. Michael and Barry return from the bathroom. They are ready to party.

4. Dom and Donna dance. They are making up.

DONNY. This next song is going out to all of you lovers out there ... A slow dance for all of you.

5. The Band plays SONG #12 (A classic rock tune. Approx. time: 2 minutes and 45 seconds.) This was Michael and Tina's song. She looks for him and finds him.

She calls him over and they dance together. This is a beautiful and awkward moment. Tony doesn't see them dancing.

6. Nunzio wants to do "socials." He goes to where Vinnie's staff is eating and tells one of them to get a tray, eight shot glasses and a vodka bottle and to follow him. They go to the Nunzio table where he dresses the caterer up as the "Toast King" by putting an apron on his head. Nunzio then goes to the bandstand.

SOCIALS: TINA AND CONNIE HAVE IT OUT

1. As SONG #12 ends, Nunzio takes the mike.

NUNZIO. (*Yells.*) Tonnnyyy! Who's the man, Tony?
TONY. You're the man.
TONY and NUNZIO. (*Singing.*) "My pa ... He makes me feel ten feet tall!"
THE GIRLS. (*Chanting.*) Socha, socha, social!

(*The BAND picks up the rhythm of the CHANT and plays along. The BRIDAL PARTY gathers around the Nunzio table where the "Toast King" is handing out shots of vodka. TINA makes the first toast.*)

TINA. Alright. To um ... Christ the King. Class of '82! [or appropriate year]
TONY and DOM. (*Toasting.*) Albert Einstein High School!

(The CHANT continues. DOMINIC takes the microphone. NUNZIO cuts off the band.)

NUNZIO. Domenica!
DOMINIC. Alright, Johnny. Come over here. This is a toast from Johnny and me. We want to wish you guys in the first year of your marriage ... May you be blessed with...
DOM and JOHNNY. Three strong, beautiful, baby, masculine, BOYS!

(EVERYONE downs a shot. NUNZIO signals the band to resume. The CHANT starts up again. Glasses are re-filled. CONNIE takes a shot glass and prepares to make a toast. NUNZIO stops the band again.)

CONNIE. OK. OK. Here's my toast for Tina. It's a poem I wrote for her ...
TINA. *(Interrupting.)* Connie. What are you doin'? You're freakin' pregnant.

(TINA grabs the shot out of Connie's hand. Defiantly, CONNIE stalks off.)

TINA. *(Following her.)* You're not a maid of honor! You're a maid of trash! Made of trash!

2. BAND STRIKES UP SONG #13 (An upbeat rock-shuffle tune. Approx. time: 2 minutes.) This is Sister's favorite song of all time. Johnny has brought the vodka from "socials" to Father Mark and is helping him to drink

a little. Sister is dancing like crazy, letting out years of pent-up personality.

3. Tina and Connie face off. Barry tries to play peacemaker. Donna adds fuel to the fire. Tina fires Connie from being maid of honor and appoints Donna in her place.

4. Barry gets Father Mark to break up Connie and Tina. Father Mark tries to "rap" with them one on one as they flip each other the finger behind his back.

THE GROUP PARTY DANCE

1. SONG #13 ENDS.

JOEY. (*From the bandstand.*) Ladies and gentlemen. It is now time for a Vitale family tradition which is ... [The name of the group party dance]

(*TINA and DONNA hear this and leave Connie in the dust.*)

DONNY. Alright! You heard the man. So everybody get out of your seats and get on the dance floor! We're gonna do this together.

(*DONNY further encourages the guests to join in. The BRIDAL PARTY all grab someone and help get people on the floor. HE begins music when EVERYONE is assembled.*)

BAND BEGINS THE GROUP PARTY DANCE. (Approx. time: 1 minute and 30 seconds.) Joey leads the dance. Nunzio has achieved the alcohol "click." Through a veil of sentimentality and regret, he looks at Mrs. Vitale. She looks beautiful.

THE INTERNATIONAL MEDLEY

1. THE BAND GOES IMMEDIATELY INTO THE "INTERNATIONAL MEDLEY." (Approx. time: 2 minutes and 30 seconds.)

DONNY. Stay on the dance floor 'cause we're gonna take you around the world without even leaving the room with the magic of music. I need everybody in one big circle. One big circle 'cause we are going to Israel. It's Hora time. Here we go! (*Singing.*) Hava Nagila! Hava Nagila!

("HAVA NAGILA"—BRIDAL PARTY and GUESTS form a large circle. TONY and TINA dance in the middle. THEY are joined by MRS. VITALE and NUNZIO, who have "sweet eyes" for each other. BARRY and MICHAEL do shots at the bar. TONY and JOHNNY end this section with a Cossack-style dance.)

DONNY. Ok. Let's go to Mexico!

(MEXICAN HAT DANCE—ALL grab a partner for the dance. The circle stays intact. NUNZIO and MRS.

VITALE do a bullfight pantomime that culminates with NUNZIO sticking Mrs. Vitale in the butt with his "horns." SHE is delighted. TINA dances with AUNT ROSE, another family tradition. TINA gives her mom some attitude and tells Joey to keep an eye on her. MICHAEL is getting very high. HE sits by himself and smiles nervously.)

DONNY. Tina and Josephina! Let's go home to Italia!

(THE TARANTELLA—TINA dances with her MOTHER. JOHNNY and TONY carry NUNZIO around the circle on their shoulders. NUNZIO beams and says, "Look at me, Josie!" SHE flirts back. THEY are acting like kids in high school. As the song ends, GRANDMA is brought out to dance with UNCLE LUI. THE SONG ENDS. NUNZIO takes MRS. VITALE by the hand to the bar.)

DONNY. We want to thank you for traveling on our Fusion Jet. I hope no one has any trouble getting through customs. If you know what I mean.

STILETTOS

1. Dom yells "Stilettos" [The name of the old street gang] and the call is taken up by Johnny and Tony.

TONY, DOM, JOHNNY. (*Chanting.*) STILETTOS! Uh, uh. Rule the streets. Uh, uh. STILETTOS!

*(THEY chant up and down the dance floor as the GIRLS
taunt them saying: "Assholes.")*

2. Johnny encourages the band to play a raucous "party
hearty" song.

3. BAND STRIKES UP Song #15 (Approx. time: 2
minutes and 30 seconds.) As they rev up for the first
chorus, Johnny prepares to do a stomach-slide on the dance
floor. He does it.

4. Michael and Barry slam-dance as Johnny, Tony and
Dom dance around à la "Animal House." Nunzio has gotten
Mrs. Vitale to have a drink with him and has placed his
carnation in her bosom.

5. Nunzio brings a bottle of vodka from the bar onto
the dance floor and all the guys compete to take the biggest
swig. Michael takes the biggest monster swig of them all,
encouraged by Nunzio.

6. Tina yells at Michael for drinking. Tony is lifted up
onto Johnny and Dom's shoulders and is carried around the
circle. Nunzio hands the bottle of vodka to Tony.

7. The devil has entered Michael. He is exuberant, and
reaches up to grab the bottle from Tony just as he is taking
a swig. The bottle smacks Tony's mouth.

8. Michael takes off with the vodka bottle with Tony,
Dom and Barry in pursuit. They chase him around the
reception hall, music still going. Tina and the girls are
freaking out. Tony catches Michael as he bursts back into
the circle.

9. Tony threatens Michael as SONG ENDS.

DONNY. Thank you! Alright, folks. Things look like they are getting a little hot out there on the dance floor. And from where I stand it looks a little too hot.

10. Barry comes to Michael's aid. Tony questions Barry as to whose best man he really is; his or Michael's?

11. Tina has her first emergency as a married woman. She runs back to the bar: "Give me a shot for my husband!"

DONNY. Someone just told me that apparently we have something special in store for you so why don't we slow down the pace, find our seats and take a breather.

12. Nunzio lets out a rebel yell and goes to the Vitale table, vodka bottle in hand.

13. Tina arrives and feeds Tony the shot. She takes him away to cool him down. She yells at Michael and tells Barry to get Michael out.

14. Barry takes Michael to a private corner, where Michael begs Barry for a pint of tequila.

VINNIE'S STAND-UP ACT

1. DONNY. Alright, folks. We have something very special in store for you. I'm gonna reintroduce someone you've already met tonight. But you're gonna see this dude in a very different light. Ladies and gentlemen ... The comedy stylings of Mr. Vinnie Black!

(VINNIE takes the microphone as his FAMILY stands behind him acting as a human applause sign for his routine.)

VINNIE. Alright. Where are all the Italians out there tonight? You know the Italians are wonderful people? They really throw great weddings, but the Italians can't fight. You know why the Italians lost the war? Because they used spaghetti instead of shells! (*Rim shot from the drummer.*) I love the Italians. Hey, does anybody know how Tony got his name? I'll tell ya how Tony got his name. When he came over on the boat they stamped his head "To New York"! (*Rimshot.*) Where are all my Jewish friends out here tonight? We got any Jewish people? Hey, did you hear the story about the little Jewish boy? Little Jewish boy gets a part in a play at school. He comes home from school and says, "Ma, I just got a great part in a play." She says, "What part did you get?" He says, "I got the part of a Jewish husband." She says, "Go back and tell them you want a speaking part!" I tell you ...Where's Mary? Where's my birthday girl? Stand up. Seventy-five years old today. Let's give her a hand. I tell you if they put the right number of candles on your cake, Mary, it would be a fire hazard! Let's hear it for the catering staff. Weren't they beautiful? Hey, did you hear the story about the two little old ladies? They're sittin' on the porch ... one goes to the other one. She says, "Thank God it's Friday. My husband's coming home with a bunch of roses for me!" The other one says, "Jesus, if my husband came home with roses, I'd have to lay on my back with my feet up in the air." The other one says, "What? You don't have a vase?" Hey, I'm opening up a new restaurant. You're all invited. It's gonna be on [name of a local street]. It's Kosher/Japanese. You know what I'm gonna call it? SO SUE ME! (*Rimshot.*)

NOTE: Any additional jokes are welcome as long as the monologue doesn't exceed three minutes.

(*The following occurs during VINNIE'S MONOLOGUE.*)

2. Nunzio and Mrs. Vitale steal away to a more private place.

3. Barry scores a pint of tequila at the bar for Michael. He puts it under his coat, takes Michael to a secluded spot, and hands the bottle over. Michael drinks deeply from it.

4. Dom and Donna furiously "make out" underneath the dais table.

5. As Vinnie nears the end of his act, Marina tells Tina that something is going on between Mrs. Vitale and Nunzio. Tina high-tails it to where they are.

6. Michael, with bottle hidden under his coat, laughs until he nearly cries at a very dumb joke of Vinnie's.

7. Nunzio and Mrs. Vitale are giggling like school-kids. Tina gets a load of the carnation in her bosom and goes off the deep end.

8. Tina and her mother reach the Vitale table as Vinnie is finishing up his act.

9. Mrs. Vitale's family, led by Tina, reprimand her for her trampy behavior. Uncle Lui takes it all in.

SANTA LUCIA

1.VINNIE. And now, my friends, I wanna bring up a
very beautiful woman and not only is she a beautiful
woman—she happens to be a beautiful singer.

TINA. (*Screaming across the room.*) Donna?

*(DOM and DONNA come up for air from underneath the
dais. DOM has lipstick all over his face. THEY go back
down.)*

VINNIE. No. Your mother, Mrs. Josephina Vitale. And
ladies and gentlemen, we have another treat, Uncle Lui is
gonna tinkle on the piano. (*VINNIE hands the mike to
MRS. VITALE.*)

MRS. VITALE. (*On the mike.*) Come on, Lui.

*(TINA and SISTER ALBERT MARIA escort UNCLE LUI
to the piano.)*

MRS. VITALE. Let's have a round of applause for
Vinnie Black. I would like, at this moment, to dedicate a
special song to a very special man in this room. This song
I used to sing for my daughter when she was a baby and I
used to sing it for my Joey and Teresa, too. And tonight,
I'd like to sing it for Tony. To welcome him into the
family. Properly. Nicely. Now, my Uncle Lui has been
practicing with me all week so I know it's gonna go good.
The song is "Santa Lucia." And any of you who know the
words sing along. It's good luck. If you please, Uncle Lui,
"Santa Lucia."

2. Mrs. Vitale sings "SANTA LUCIA" (Approx. time: 1 minute), accompanied by Uncle Lui.

3. Joey, Sister and Tina stand behind her with their arms around each other, swaying. Tony encourages applause from guests. Tina and Sister Albert Maria start waltzing together, something they've done since they were little girls.

4. When the song is about half finished, Tony falls to his knees in front of Mrs. Vitale yelling: "Mamma! Mamma!" He is joined by Barry, Dom and Johnny.

5. Michael tries to be funny by howling and pumping his leg like a dog who is trying to scratch an unreachable itch.

6. Tina decides it would be fun to make Terry dizzy. So, she spins her around in a circle.

7. Mrs. Vitale has a big finish, and hugs Tony. Uncle Lui doesn't know the song is over and Tina goes to him to tell him to stop.

MRS. VITALE. And I'd like a special round of applause for Uncle Lui. (*To Uncle Lui.*) Stand up and take a bow.

8. As Lui gets up he falls against the keyboard making a terrible sound. Mrs. Vitale blames Tina for Uncle Lui's fall. Their battle continues as Tina snaps back with a look that could kill. Lui is helped off the bandstand by Tina and Joey. Nunzio staggers to the bar followed by Johnny, Dom and Tony. Michael, on a real roll, attempts to amuse Tony with his "No more Rice Krispies" Pavarotti singing bit.

THE DOLLAR DANCE

1. Mrs. Vitale holds on to the mike and announces "The Dollar Dance."

MRS. VITALE. *(Re: Uncle Lui.)* Alright. He's Ok. Bring him down 'cause we got one more surprise. Not just for my Tony, but for my daughter, too. They don't know about it. There's a tradition in our family that we're gonna continue with, tonight. Now, you know the bride and groom are getting ready to leave us to go on their honeymoon—to [name of a very tacky honeymoon spot]! So, we're gonna do a Dollar Dance!

(TINA refuses to do it, saying: "No way. It's retarded." SHE heads back to the bar for a shot.)

MRS. VITALE. *(Re: Tina.)* She's gonna do it. Get her up here! She wants to do it. Go get her, Marina.

(MARINA runs to the bar to get Tina.)

MRS. VITALE. Now, all you have to do is reach into your pockets and take out money and pin it on the bride and groom. That's what a Dollar Dance is.

(TONY comes onto the dance floor.)

MRS. VITALE. We got the groom! We're gonna line up behind the bride or the groom and pin the money on them. A dollar, five, ten, twenty, one hundred—the sky's the limit. Tina? Tina? Get up here. (*Screams like a condor.*) TINA!!! GET UP HERE NOW!

(*Nothing can save Tina. SHE gives in as AUNT ROSE leads her to the dance floor.*)

MRS. VITALE. Thank you, Rose, for bringing *my* daughter up to me. Ladies and gentlemen, line up for the Dollar Dance!

(*TINA's eyes shoot poison darts at her mother.*)

2. DONNY. Alright, folks. Before we get started, it was brought to my attention, during the dinner break, that one of our bridesmaids used to sing in a band called "Strumpet." And she would like to offer the gift of song to Tony and Tina. Come on up here, Donna Marsala!

(*TINA runs from her place and hugs Donna. TINA brings her to the bandstand and instructs Rick to tape her for "Star Search." SHE helps DONNA with a few pieces of choreography for the song before UNCLE LUI calls her back in line.*)

3. Rose hands out pins to Connie and Barry who will be the first to dance with Tina and Tony.

4. BAND PLAYS SONG # 14 (A MEDLEY of "uplifting" ballads. Approx. time: 6 to 9 minutes.) with Donna on lead vocals. Dom hates this. Sal and Rick get pics/video.

5. During the first song of the medley, Tony dances with all takers easily and with charm. Tina, however, has a

rough time. Things start well as Uncle Lui comes up and pins a twenty dollar bill on her for his dance. Tina leaves him hanging as she runs to her mother saying: "Look, Mommy. Uncle Lui gave me twenty dollars." He beams as he dances with Tina. As they dance, Nunzio cuts to the front of the line where Johnny was waiting his turn.

6. Before the proud glow can fade from Lui's cheeks, Nunzio washes up holding five twenties in the air. He announces: "One hundred dollars!" He is too drunk to pin the money on with ease. He finally does, then stumbles through a dance, handling Tina a little familiarly. Mrs. Vitale comes to her aid. Nunzio tries to kiss Mrs. Vitale, who is getting disgusted with him. Nunzio staggers to the Vitale table and plants himself there. Johnny steps up to dance with Tina.

7. Father Mark is drunk, and Sister is giving him hell. Johnny finishes his dance, and Tina's problems continue. Michael is next. He is very maudlin about their past, and wants to talk about it. Tina is not in the mood. He is obviously very high. She motions for Connie to get rid of him. She does, but Michael cuts back in the line for another turn.

8. During the second song of the medley, Sister gets Dominic to help with Father Mark. It's useless. He's too far gone. Sister confesses her love for Dom. From the bandstand, Donna is well aware of what's going on. Dom decides to give Sister a dose of reality by kissing her. Sister runs away in shock.

9. Nunzio is having a talk with Mrs. Vitale that is part dreams, part regrets and mostly booze. He orders Johnny, who is talking at the next table, to get him a beer. Johnny says something that Nunzio hears as an insult and he

smacks Johnny across the head. Johnny flares and takes off to the bar. Rose and Mrs. Vitale are shocked. Nunzio drags himself after Johnny. Michael cuts in line to dance with Tina yet again. This time, he wants to let Tina know that he still loves her. She's not interested.

10. Michael dances with Tina for a third time. He is a little more high, desperate and forceful. Tony sees that Tina is in trouble and comes to her rescue. He pulls Michael's headband from behind. Michael turns around and sees Sal. Thinking Sal was his attacker, Michael assumes a Kung Fu pose, threatening to fight. Meanwhile, Tina goes off to dance with Tony. Barry comes and takes Michael to a quiet table. As the song ends, Tony and Tina finish the dance with Tina putting a dollar bill in Tony's pants.

DONNY. Let's hear it for the gorgeous Ms. Donna Marsala!
DONNA. Thank you.

NOTE: Three songs may be needed if many people want to dance with Tony and Tina. If not, everything in this beat can be played in two songs.

THE MUSIC VIDEO

1. Joey has arranged for Donny to announce that he and the girls will re-create their lip-sync version of a music video Joey has choreographed.

2. DONNY. Apparently, there's a celebrity among us tonight and she's standing right here in the white dress.

(DONNY crosses to TINA who is at the Vitale table with MARINA unpinning her dollars. SHE relishes her haul.)

DONNY. Tina, what would you say to me if I said to you, Paula Abdul? [OR NAME OF A POPULAR SINGER]

TINA. Shut up.

DONNY. Well, what would you say to your brother, Joey, if he had said to you ...

JOEY. COLD HEARTED SNAKE! [OR NAME OF POPULAR SONG BY A FEMALE SINGER]

TINA. I'd tell him to shut up, too, 'cause I'm not doin' it, Joey.

DONNY. Tina, we have the tape.

TINA. *(Loving it.)* Joey, you dick.

DONNY. Apparently, Tina and her girlfriends won a "puttin' on the hits" dance contest at Sparks Disco with a number her brother choreographed. I think with some encouragement from you, we can get her to do it for us now!

(AUDIENCE cheers. TINA, DONNA, CONNIE, and MARINA act mortified at the idea of doing this. In reality, they can't wait.)

TINA. (*"If you really want me too ..."*) Alright. I'll do it.

(The GIRLS get in position for the dance.)

DONNY. I give you Tina and her Snake Girls!
MRS. VITALE. Smile, Tina!

3. Donny puts on a cassette tape of the song. Rick DeMarco films the entire dance as if he were Martin Scorcese.

4. As the girls dance, Joey blows a fan in their faces for a "special effect."

5. Nunzio gathers up five beers to bring to the Vitale table as a peace offering. He makes the perilous journey across the dance floor, dodging the girls as they perform and barely managing the beers. Tina tries to hold it together. At the table, the Vitales try to get Nunzio to sit down, but he wants to do a dance for Mrs. Vitale instead. Tina sees Nunzio with her mother and tells Joey to take care of it. Joey finishes his part of the dance and approaches Nunzio who begins to dance with him. The girls finish the dance even though it has been spoiled by Nunzio. Tina comes to her mother's table and thanks her for ruining her dance. She storms off, very pissed. She has to find Barry. He has the only thing that can make her happy at this point—lines of cocaine.

MADDY DANCES ON THE BAR/
MRS. VITALE CATCHES TINA

1. DONNY. Alright, folks. Let's get up and boogie. This one goes out to all you beautiful women out there.

(BAND BEGINS SONG #15 (An up-tempo dance tune. Approx. time: 1 minute and 30 seconds.)

2. Connie finds Barry and sits down. Tina approaches Barry's table and asks for a couple of lines of coke. She then begs a vial off Barry, who obliges. Tina tears off to "turn on" her friends, who are dancing. She proceeds to get very high.

3. Johnny and Dom encourage Maddy to do a sexy dance on top of the bar. Nunzio is dancing alone on the floor. He sees Maddy and stumbles to the bar.

4. Seeing Maddy, Mrs. Vitale makes a bee-line for the bar. Everything is falling apart. She pulls Maddy down while Nunzio hounds her for being "no fun" and "old." Tony tries to smooth things over. THE SONG ENDS.

DONNY. This next song goes out to you, the family and friends of Tony and Tina.

(BAND PLAYS SONG #16 (An up-tempo rock anthem. Approx. time: 1 minute and 15 seconds.)

6. Maddy is unabashed. She grabs Johnny and starts a "Love Train" that snakes around the reception hall. Michael sits alone at the dais, watching everyone dance. He vomits behind the dais. He feels very hot and unbuttons his shirt.

7. No sooner has Mrs. Vitale stamped one fire out, another flares up. She spots Tina on the bandstand spooning cocaine to the band. Tina is very high. Mrs. Vitale heads for Tina.

8. Tina sees her coming, and is terrified. She runs. Mrs. Vitale chases Tina. Mrs. Vitale traps Tina in a corner. The only thing between them are two tables. Tina is like a frightened little girl. Mrs. Vitale demands, "Get over here!" Tina doesn't move. Mrs. Vitale goes on, "I'm gonna give you to the count of three. One. Two. Three!" Tina still doesn't move. Mrs. Vitale is fed up. "Alright. That's it." Mrs. Vitale crosses to the bandstand.

DADDY'S LITTLE GIRL/ MICHAEL'S ATTACK

1. Mrs. Vitale is determined to regain control of the wedding. She STOPS SONG #16 by taking the mike from Donny. The "Love Train" people are mad about the interruption and jeer Mrs. Vitale. She is undaunted:

MRS. VITALE. (*Slowly, almost sadistic.*) Clear the dance floor! At this time, my daughter has a special request. She would like to dance for her late father with her brother, Joey.
TINA. You're sick, Ma!

2. Tina hates her mother right now. Joey knows it is futile to argue so he calms Tina down. Michael's head is throbbing and reeling.
3. BAND PLAYS SONG #17 (A sweet father/daughter song. Approx. time: 15 seconds.) Tina and Joey dance. Tina is crying.

4. Michael, in another world, approaches the bandstand and gets Donny in his sights. He tears off his shirt, throwing it at Donny. He presses his attack and throws Donny to the ground, grabbing the mike. The song stops abruptly.

5. Michael takes the floor and pathetically belts out a phrase from a heavy-metal song. On his bare chest is a tattoo with the inscription: "TINA—R.I.P." Tina sees the tattoo and faints.

6. Donny recovers and wrestles Michael to the ground as Johnny, Barry and Dom arrive on the scene and pull them apart. Tony comes to Tina's aid, and lifts her into a chair. Marina runs to get Tina a glass of water.

7. THE BAND PLAYS SONG #18, (a love ballad. Approx. time: 1 minute and 15 seconds.) The song seems ironic at this time. Barry, Dom and Johnny escort Michael out of the hall. Nunzio follows, encouraging Michael to fight.

8. Tony lifts Tina out of her chair and spins her around as they kiss. Tina gets carried away and starts to undo Tony's pants. Tony is uncomfortable. Uncle Lui is watching and can't take it. He reprimands Tina. He tells Tina that she is acting like a baby. Tina responds by loudly proclaiming that Uncle Lui is a baby because he "wears a diaper." Uncle Lui slaps her. Tony is mad at Tina. Tina, like a spoiled brat, shouts an insincere apology to Uncle Lui.

CUTTING THE CAKE

1. DONNY. Alright, folks. Join me as we serenade this beautiful couple in the cutting of the cake.

(Vinnie's STAFF brings out the wedding cake. TONY and TINA get ready to cut it. TINA is very high and TONY is still mad. SHE makes believe she's "Jason" from "Friday the 13th." JOHNNY tries to calm Tina down.)

2. THE BAND PLAYS "THE BRIDE CUTS THE CAKE" and everyone sings along. Tina stabs the top layer of the cake with the knife, causing it to slide off. Loretta saves it, and puts a piece on a plate for Tina.

3. Tina flirts with Dom shamelessly, saying she wants a kiss. Tina takes a forkful of cake but instead of feeding it to Tony, she tries to feed it to Dom. Dom guides her to her husband's mouth. Tony eats the cake. He is pissed. Vinnie gives Tony the knife to cut the cake. He cuts a big piece.

4. DONNY. OK, Tony. The bigger the piece, the happier the marriage!

(TONY takes his piece of cake and makes like he's going to feed it to Tina. SHE opens her mouth and at the last moment, HE shoves the cake in Tina's face. SHE runs off to the bathroom followed by MARINA, DONNA and CONNIE. DOM and JOHNNY high-five Tony. THEY lift him on their shoulders and throw him up in the air three times.)

5. Mrs. Vitale follows Tina to the bathroom. Vinnie requests Tina's presence to throw the bouquet. Tony takes the mike:

TONY. Tina, get your ass out here right now!

DONNA. (*Entering from bathroom.*) She's not comin' out, Tony, so just dream about it!

TONY. Oh, is that right? (*HE grabs his crotch.*) I got your dream right here!

6. Donna screams and runs toward the bathroom. Tony tears after her, tossing the mike to Vinnie. The guys yell and hoot in macho encouragement.

7. Mrs. Vitale emerges from the bathroom with cake all over her face.

THE BOUQUET AND GARTER

1. VINNIE. Can we have all the single ladies up here for the throwing of the bouquet?

The single ladies gather to catch the bouquet as Tony carries Tina, slung across his shoulder, onto the dance floor. Connie helps Mrs. Vitale wipe away the cake. Marina and Donna follow Tony, giving him hell. Mrs. Vitale separates Tina from Tony and drags her across the dance floor, insisting that she throw the bouquet. Tina is out of control.

2. BAND PLAYS A SEXY BASS RIFF. Tina shrieks, "All right! I'll throw the freakin' bouquet!" Tina falls in Donny's arms. He helps put her in position and helps her throw the bouquet. Tina finds Donny sexy and starts kissing him on the neck.

3. A chair is brought out and Donny sits Tina in it for the Garter ceremony THE BAND PLAYS STRIPPER MUSIC. (Approx. time: 30 seconds.) Tony kneels in front of Tina to remove the garter. She plants her foot in his chest. When he gets the garter off her leg, she flips him the finger and nods out in the chair. Aunt Rose gets her up. Tina pushes her away and stumbles to the gift table.

4. VINNIE. Now can we get all the single guys up here, please?

(BAND PLAYS A SURFING RIFF as Tony throws a fake-out. A moment later, Tony throws the garter for real. Throughout, he never takes his eyes off Tina. As soon as the garter leaves his hand, he is off to the gift table.)

5. Vinnie gets the woman who caught the bouquet and the guy who caught the garter together. BAND plays STRIPPER MUSIC AGAIN as the guy puts the garter on the woman.

6. Tony reaches the gift table and asks Tina "What is the matter?" She says, "I want my father." They argue. Tina, in a drunken tantrum, smacks the gifts off the table. Tony has had enough. He says, "I'm outta here."

7. Tony storms out of the reception hall. Barry is afraid he's not coming back and follows.

8. Tina passes out. Donna, Marina and Connie carry her to a bar stool. Donna tries to calm her down by singing to

her. Tina vomits into a napkin. Connie starts gagging as well.

9. Barry catches up with Tony just outside the reception hall. Tony is pissed. Barry talks Tony into staying at the reception and not "divorcing" Tina. They discuss this until they hear Marina's frantic cries for Tony to save the day.

MADELINE STRIPS

1. BAND BEGINS SONG #17 (A funky dance song. Approx. time: 1 minute and 15 seconds.)

2. Nunzio and Maddy take to the dance floor. Maddy does a sexy dance for Nunzio. It turns into a dance for the whole crowd. Johnny moves people back to give her room. Encouraged by Nunzio, this naturally becomes a striptease. Tina, through her drunken stupor, sees Maddy dancing. She staggers to the dance floor.

3. Mrs. Vitale sees what's going on, and is horrified. She goes to the bandstand to try and get the band to stop the music. Nunzio unzips Maddy's dress and pulls it down. Marina runs to get Tony.

4. Mrs. Vitale grabs Nunzio from behind. Nunzio wheels around and pushes Mrs. Vitale to the floor. Tina jumps on Nunzio's back and forces him to the ground, biting him. The band stops the music.

5. Dom pulls Tina off Nunzio as Tony and Barry rush in. Loretta Black runs to Mrs. Vitale's aid. Johnny and Joey begin to fight as Tony "cools everybody out."

TONY. Cool the fuck out! Dad, this is a wedding hall, not a strip joint! And Johnny, you oughtta know better!

JOHNNY. What'd I do?

TONY. You were born. (*To Mrs. Vitale.*) And Ma, I love you. And I know you don't like my family. Get off the floor 'cause I know you're not hurt.

(*MRS. VITALE sits up as TONY focuses in on Tina.*)

TONY. Is this the wedding you wanted? I got the flashbulbs going off in my eyes. I got the video guy up my ass. (*Re: Father Mark.*) I got Father Happy Hour here. Look at him. I thought getting married was about getting married, honey. Not all this bullshit! Sorry I spit on ya. I love you, Tina. You know? I love you.

TINA. (*Straightening up.*) I love you too, Tony.

(*TINA runs to him. SHE feels embarrassed and just wants to leave with her husband.*)

6. Tony sends Tina to get changed into her honeymoon outfit. Marina helps her. As they leave, Mr. Nunzio calls Mrs. Vitale "a fat ass." Mrs. Vitale runs screaming toward Mr. Nunzio. She wants to choke him, but her family pulls her away. The families trade insults as they go to their tables. Tony throws his hands in the air as he goes to get Tina.

THE FINAL PHOTOGRAPH

1. BAND PLAYS SONG #18 (A classic rock ballad. Approx. time: 2 minutes and 30 seconds.) with Donna singing. She introduces the song with the following dedication: "This is Tina's favorite song."

2. Sal gathers the families on the dance floor for a family photo. This is no small feat, but with the cooler heads prevailing all are finally assembled just as the song ends.

3. As Tony and Tina enter, Sal asks them to get into the picture. They refuse. They've had enough.

4. Tina kisses Uncle Lui goodbye as the families try and get Tony and Tina to join in the picture.

5. As Tony and Tina leave, Sal, ready to snap the photo, asks everyone to say "*La Famiglia*." Disgusted, Uncle Lui retorts, "*Va fa culo*." Sal snaps the picture.

TONY AND TINA DEPART

1. THE BAND STRIKES UP SONG #19 (An upbeat "farewell" song. Approx. time: 1 minute and 45 seconds.)

VINNIE. Alright, folks. Let's wish Tony and Tina our best.

(*MUSIC starts up. It's Vinnie Black's theme song.*)

DONNY. Ladies and gentlemen, Mr. Vinnie Black!

(VINNIE sings.)

2. The bridal party and the Vitale family follow Tony and Tina to their car. The Nunzios slip away, dragging Father Mark. Tina runs to Uncle Lui to apologize again and kisses him goodbye. He gives her all the dollar dance money. She kisses the rest of her family and, exhausted, walks to the car.

3. Tina can't get in the car. It is stuffed with balloons. She pops them with her cigarette to make room.

4. Tony and Tina crank up the stereo and pull away as the guests throw rice.

5. Dom and Donna fight over how they're going to get home since Tony and Tina have Dom's car.

6. Barry invites everyone to come to his house to continue the party.

7. The audience leaves. The wedding is over.

THE END

PRODUCTION NOTES

AUDITIONS

The most important quality to look for when casting The Wedding is the actors ability to improv well, be natural and have a sense of humor. Below are suggested audition improvisations. Please feel free to create your own as well.

1. FOR TONY AND TINA—the proposal.

2. FOR MRS. VITALE AND TINA —It is two weeks before the wedding and the morning of Tina's bridal gown fitting. Much to Mrs. Vitale's disgust, Tina's hung over and doesn't want to go.

3. FOR NUNZIO AND MADDY—She's trying out a new dance for the strip club for Nunzio.

4. FOR BARRY, DOM AND MICHAEL—Dom tries to buy pot from Barry who has unfortunately sold his last joint to Michael. Dom has to beg Michael for it.

5. FOR TINA, DONNA, MARINA AND CONNIE—It's 3:30 a.m. Tony, Dom and Barry are late picking the girls up from Sparks Disco. They wait on the sidewalk, and Marina is wasted.

6. FOR JOEY AND RICK—Joey tells Rick he can come to the wedding not as his boyfriend *but* as the videographer.

7. FOR SAL, TINA, MRS.V—The ladies pay a visit to Sal to see if he's got what it takes to photograph the wedding.

8. FOR CONNIE, BARRY—Connie tells Barry that she's pregnant and that she doesn't want to get married.

9. FOR FATHER MARK, TONY, TINA—A "Pre-Cana" session where they talk about sexuality.

10. FOR VINNIE, LORETTA, TONY AND TINA—Tony and Tina stop in on the Blacks to set the date for their reception, get a tour of the Coliseum and talk money.

11. FOR SISTER ALBERT, TINA, MRS. VITALE AND UNCLE LUI—Terry tells her family she wants to be a nun.

12. FOR UNCLE LUI AND NUNZIO—Nunzio offends Uncle Lui by offering to pay for half the wedding.

13. FOR JOHNNY, GRANDMA, TONY AND NUNZIO—Nunzio and Johnny fight over Johnnie's unwillingness to follow his dad's orders. Grandma comforts Johnny.

14. FOR JOEY AND MARINA—Joey tells Marina he's gay and not in love with her.

15. FOR DOM, DONNA—Donna has an audition for Star Search and dumps Dominic and their weekend plans.

16. FOR AUNT ROSE AND MRS. VITALE—Mrs. V. is jealous of Rose's close relationship with Tina.

17. FOR VINNIE BLACK—Vinnie tells a few jokes to show off his stand-up abilities.

18. FOR DONNY DULCE—Donny sings to show off his range and "hip" style.

I. REHEARSAL PROCESS

Tony 'n' Tina's Wedding has a very exciting and different rehearsal process. For what each company will attempt to do is create a very detailed and specific world that the audience is invited to enter. In effect, the audience creates the world with you—there is no fourth wall.

Through the history sessions and the improvisations, you
will create a history for your character that cannot be
shaken by any audience member. It is important to have a
pact amongst the company to *never break character under
any circumstances*. This will create a rock solid unity that
will draw the audience into your reality. Prior to the first
rehearsal, it is important that each actor has become
familiar with the time line and each other's character
biographies. Special attention should be paid to the Vitale-
Nunzio "bad blood" story included in Uncle Lui's bio.

II. REHEARSAL SCHEDULE – based on 8 hours
a day/6 days a week

DAY ONE

This day is devoted to creating the history of Tony and
Tina's world. This is accomplished in two ways:

The Field Trip. Take a few hours to explore the
neighborhood and surrounding areas where the wedding will
be performed. Find your school, your church, the bars you
hang out in, etc. Where's the mall? The Mini-mall? Where
do you live?—you get the idea.

History Session. This is very important in creating an
absolute reality for Tony and Tina. *It is crucial for all the
actors to know the history*. This isn't just actor homework.
Unlike other forms of theater, the audience will be talking
to you and asking you questions. The same questions they
may ask other actors. Some may even try to stump you. If
stories don't jibe, it not only weakens the reality of the

play, it also makes you look stupid. However, this doesn't mean that the characters, like all people, don't have selective memories, or their own versions of the "truth." But it is essential that everyone start on common ground.

Below are some questions you should answer as a company, and then make your bible for performance. It may be appropriate for some characters *not* to know the answers to some of these questions, or certain parts of the history. If this is the case, *make it known*. This kind of consistency pays off.

1. How old are you?
2. Where do you live?
3. What's your occupation?
4. What schools have you attended? Did you graduate?
5. What kind of car do you drive?
6. Have you ever been to Nunzio's strip joint before?
7. Have you been to Vinnie Black's Coliseum before?
8. When is Connie and Barry's baby due?
9. Do you know Joey is gay?
10. How did Vito Vitale (Tina's father) die?
11. When did Tina date Michael and when did they break up?
12. What's the story behind Michael going to rehab?
13. What happened to Vi Nunzio (Tony's mother)?
14. Have you heard Donny Dulce and Fusion before?
15. Do you know about Joey and Rick's relationship?
16. When and where did Tony propose to Tina?
17. Who's paying for what at the wedding?
18. What did you do the night before the wedding?
19. What is your wedding gift to Tony and Tina?
20. Where are Tony and Tina going on their honeymoon?

DAY TWO

CHOREOGRAPHY
First Dance, SONG #14, International Medley, SONG #15, Champagne March, Music Video and Maddy's Strip.

And when not learning dances:

IMPROV
1. <u>Confessions</u> with Father Mark: Entire cast.
Each cast member takes a turn going to confession with Father Mark.
2. <u>High School Flashback</u>
Tina's house – bedroom.
Tina, Donna, Marina and Terry (Sr. Albert Maria) are having a high school sleep-over which Michael crashes with two six-packs of beer.
3. <u>Tony Asks Mrs. Vitale For Tina's Hand</u>
Mrs. Vitale's kitchen.
Tony, Tina, Mrs. Vitale and Joey.

DAY THREE

BLOCK
"Pre-ceremony" through "Ceremony"

IMPROV
<u>Tina and Tony's Jack and Jill Bridal Shower.</u>

Mrs. Vitale's house.
CAST, except Michael, Donny D., Rick and Sal.

DAY FOUR

BLOCK
"Receiving Line" through "Grandma Falls"

IMPROV
Tina Has Fight With Mom and Decides To Move In
With Tony At His Dad's House.

Nunzio's house.
Tina, Tony, Nunzio, Grandma, Johnny, Dom and
Maddy.

DAY FIVE

BLOCK
"Pictures for the Mantlepiece" through "Blessing of the
Food"

IMPROV
Party At Connie And Barry's

Connie and Barry's apartment.
Tony, Tina, Dom, Donna, Connie, Barry, Johnny,
Marina, Joey, Rick, Michael.

DAY SIX

BLOCK
Dinner One through "Socials"

EVENING IMPROV

CAST goes bowling in public—in character.

DAY SEVEN

BLOCK
"SONG #13" through "Santa Lucia"

IMPROV
Tina's Father's Wake

Vitale house – after the night viewing.

FULL CAST

DAY EIGHT

BLOCK
"Dollar Dance" through "SONG #16"

IMPROV
Rehearsal Dinner

Nunzio's Bar

Bridal party, families and Father Mark.

DAY NINE

BLOCK
"Cutting the Cake" through END

<u>IMPROV</u>
<u>The Morning of The Wedding</u>

1. Vitale house.

Tina, Uncle Lui, Mrs. Vitale, Joey, Donna, Marina, Aunt Rose, Connie.

2. Nunzio house.

Nunzio, Tony, Johnny, Dom, Grandma, Maddy, Barry.

DAY TEN

Run Thru with music.

DAY ELEVEN

Run Thru with music.

DAY TWELVE

A.M.: Run Thru with music
P.M.: Dress Rehearsal

<u>IMPORTANT NOTE:</u> Start each rehearsal with a quick run thru of all the blocking learned in prior rehearsals.

PROP LIST

CEREMONY: (PRESET)
1 candle holder w/ Bic lighter, SR
1 candle holder w/ Bic lighter, SL
1 candle holder, C
3 candles
1 podium mic
1 empty purse on chair in congregation (to save seat for Michael)
1 guitar

CEREMONY: (PERSONAL PROPS)
Missalette (Father Mark)
Bible (Father Mark)
Video camera (Rick)
Video tape (Rick)
Camera w/ flash unit (Sal)
Religious folk song dittos (Sister Albert Maria)
Bouquets (3 bridesmaids, 1 bride)
Pitch pipe (Sister Albert Maria)
Basket with boutonnieres (7 w/ pins)
Vodka bottle in plastic bag (Nunzio)

RECEPTION ROOM: (PRESET)
3 shot glasses
2 tequila bottles (pints) w/ water
2 vodka bottles (fifths) w/ water and spouts
10 beer bottles (brown) w/ water
3 Perrier waters (small)
4 champagne bottles w/ ginger ale
1 Beefeater gin bottle (spout)

1 Broadsword (Vinnie - champagne march)

VITALE TABLE: (PRESET)
1 pin cushion w/ "dollar dance" pins
5 chairs
2 ashtrays
Papal blessing (should be set near table)

DAIS: (PRESET)
2 wedding goblets (bride and groom)
1 bridal bag (Tina for "boosta" envelopes)
5 ashtrays
8 plastic champagne glasses

BANDSTAND: (PRESET)
Business cards (Donny Dulce and Fusion)

BUFFET TABLE: (PRESET)
2 warming trays
Sterno
3 baskets with forks
4 metal serving spoons
2 plastic salad tongs
1 small fire extinguisher
3 sets oven mitts
Goblet (Tina's olives)
Olives-large, black, pitted
Extra napkins
1 roll paper towels
Paper plates
Napkins

CATERING TABLE: (PRESET)
Trash bags
4 white towels (champagne pouring)
1 roll paper towels
1 bottle spray cleaner
"Socials" tray: 10 shot glasses, 1 bottle Absolut vodka (w/ spout)
Cake trays: 10
Cake server
1 throw bouquet
Kleenex
First aid kit
Cake plates
Cake forks
Sparklers or flashlights: 4 small, 1 large (champagne march)

PERSONAL PROPS: (PRESET, DRESSING ROOM)
Nunzio: 10 one dollar bills (tipping), 4 twenty-dollar bills (dollar dance)
Barry: 2 one-dollar bills, 2 small bags "cocaine" (baby laxative), 4 bogus joints
Tina: Gum, cigarettes, garter
Joey: 5 one-dollar bills (dollar dance)
Rick: Video camera equipment
Michael: 2 one-dollar bills
Donna: Bubble gum
Sal: Camera
Mrs. Vitale: Family photo album

TONY 'N' TINA'S WEDDING: THE FOOD

THE MENU

Appetizers: Ritz crackers with cheddar cheese spread

The toast: A glass of champagne

The meal: Vegetarian baked ziti, tossed salad, sliced Italian bread

The cake: Wedding cake

The food at TONY N' TINA'S WEDDING is a vital contribution to the reality of the play. Needless to say, it must be fresh and of the highest quality possible. Remember, if the food is bad, the entire cast suffers from the complaints of the audience.

CATERING SUPPLIES

(The following is for 200 people including the cast)

1. Appetizers: Served from the time the guests enter reception until "Introduction of the Wedding Party."

Items:
   a. Ritz crackers
   b. Cheddar cheese spread
   c. Trays to serve them on

2. The Toast: Glasses are placed on the tables before the reception begins. At the end of "The First Dance," begin pouring the champagne.

Items:
   a. Plastic champagne glasses (1 per person)
   b. Champagne

3. The Meal: The food cart should be ready by the time Father Mark blesses the food.

Items:
   a. A serving table on wheels
   b. 2 large steam trays
   c. Large silver serving spoons
   d. A very large salad bowl
   e. 2 sets of salad tongs
   f. 2 bowls for sliced bread
   g. Paper napkins
   h. Paper plates
   i. Plastic forks

4. Clean Up: When "Group Party Dance (Song #14)" begins, Vinnie's staff should clear as many tables as possible.

Items:
   a. Garbage bags

5. The Cake: Served by Vinnie's staff immediately after the cutting of the cake.

Items:
   a. Plastic forks
   b. Paper cake plates
   c. Trays to serve cake on

   Vinnie and Loretta Black plus four staff members do all the catering. The roles of the caterers are unique in that they incorporate "real work" along with their responsibility to create a character and to improvise. The dedication of the catering staff to keep a "clean Coliseum" helps solidify the world of the play to a greater degree.

SAL'S PHOTO LIST

CEREMONY

1. Tony and Barry by the Nunzio pew
2. Tony, Barry, Nunzio by the Vitale pew
3. Tony, Barry, Nunzio, Madeline by the Vitale pew
4. Bridesmaids and Tina in back of church
5. Mrs. Vitale as she walks up the aisle
6. Marina and Johnny as they walk up the aisle
7. Donna and Dominic as they walk up the aisle
8. Connie as she walks up the aisle
9. Tina and Joey several times as they walk up the aisle
10. Joey during his reading
11. Connie during her reading
12. Tony and Tina when they light the ceremonial candle
13. Tina during her reading
14. Tony during his reading
15. Tony and Tina during the vows
16. Tony and Tina during the blessing of the rings
17. Tony and Tina when they kiss as husband and wife
18. Tony and Tina as they run down the aisle
19. Final photo of entire bridal party before they go into the reception hall

INTRODUCTION OF THE WEDDING PARTY

1. Tony and Tina as they go through the canopy (twice)

THE FIRST DANCE

1. When Tony twirls Tina
2. When Tony and Tina kiss for the first time
3. When Tina shows off her wedding ring

4. Mrs. Vitale and Tony dancing

5. Nunzio and Tina dancing

6. "Papparazzi style" explosion when Tony and Tina et. al. dance in the "hugging circle"

PICTURES FOR THE MANTLEPIECE

1. Tony and Tina at the dais

2. Vitale family with Tony and Tina at the Vitale table

3. Nunzio family with Tony and Tina at the Nunzio table

4. Nunzio family minus Tina with Barry and Dom at Nunzio table

THE CHAMPAGNE MARCH

1. Pictures of the march

2. Vinnie and Loretta pouring champagne for Tony and Tina

THE TOASTS

1. Barry toasting Tony and Tina

2. Tony toasting Tina

3. Tina toasting Tony

4. Nunzio toasting Tony and Tina

5. Mrs. Vitale toasting Tony and Tina

6. Michael toasting Tony and Tina

7. Uncle Lui toasting Tony and Tina

THE PAPAL BLESSING

1. Tina holding the Papal Blessing with Terry, Joey and Tony

DINNER ONE: "NO PROSCIUTTO IN ZITI"/BREAD FIGHT

1. "Papparazzi style" of food cart being presented to Tony and Tina

DINNER TWO: PICTURES AT THE TABLES

1. Sal takes Tony and Tina around the room for group shots

THE INTERNATIONAL MEDLEY

1. Standing on a chair behind the circle of guests, Sal takes various photos

VINNIE'S STAND-UP ACT

1. Vinnie doing his routine

SANTA LUCIA

1. Mrs. Vitale singing

THE DOLLAR DANCE

1. Tina dancing with the guys
2. Tony dancing with the girls
3. Final photo of Tina and Tony with the money pinned on them

THE MUSIC VIDEO

1. Several photos through the course of the song

MADDY DANCES ON THE BAR

1. Several photos of Maddy dancing atop the bar

DADDY'S LITTLE GIRL
   1. Joey and Tina dancing together

CUTTING THE CAKE
   1. Tina cutting the cake
   2. Tina feeding cake to Tony
   3. Tony cutting the cake
   4. Tony smashing cake in Tina's face

THE BOUQUET AND GARTER
   1. Tina throwing the bouquet
   2. Tony taking Tina's garter off
   3. Tony throwing the garter
   4. Woman who catches the bouquet having the garter put on by the man who catches it

THE FINAL PHOTOGRAPH
   1. Sal's last hurrah—a photo of both families

TROUBLESHOOTING IN
TONY N' TINA'S WEDDING

This section will address certain problems in the presentation of the wedding. Because of the close proximity of audience and actor, a keen eye should be lent to securing the safety of the actors as well as the play.

DRUGS

The use of drugs (always fake of course) has been in the show since it began in the mid 80's. They are used because in the world of Tony and Tina, drugs are a reality. Not a very glamorous reality, but truthful all the same. The use of cocaine or marijuana should never be depicted in a way that would make an audience think that drugs are a good thing. It is with your discretion that you either include or exclude the drugs. If you wish to throw that part of the play out, you will need to rethink some very vital twists in the journey of Tony and Tina and their friends. If you use the drugs, you will be making a brave statement about a very controversial fabric of our society.

THE AUDIENCE VERSUS THE CAST

Ninety-eight percent of the audience is great. The other two percent is what we address in this section. There is a fine line between the audience and the cast. A line that when overstepped can disrupt the rhythm of the show. When one of the following problems arise, look for either Vinnie Black to solve the problem or find the stage manager.

entice the audience into becoming your partners in an evening of theater that will be at once unique and unforgettable.

COSTUME NOTES

TONY: White vintage 1978 LORD WEST (brand name) 100% polyester three-piece tuxedo with black trim. White vest with black buttons, a white bow-tie (with black center). Black patent leather shoes with black socks. A white pleated tuxedo shirt. ACCESSORIES: Wedding ring, red rose boutonniere.

TINA: White satin-polyester blend wedding gown with V-shaped bodice and a sweetheart neck with elastic around the shoulders. Long detachable train to be removed after the ceremony. White lace panty hose, white shoes. White lace elbow-length, fingerless gloves. Beaded headpiece with three tiered veil. White lace garter with red or blue accent. ACCESSORIES: Tina should not wear any overpowering jewelry, chokers, etc. She can wear simple pearl and glass clip-on earrings, and simple gold necklace with charms like "Tina" or "TNT", etc. Bracelets are ok, but keep them thin and simple. GOING AWAY OUTFIT: Black Capri-length spandex slacks, ankle-length laced black boots with a pointy toe and thin heel. Cotton black and white, off-the-shoulder, zebra-print long-sleeved top. Should be skin tight. Hair gathered to one side with matching fabric hair clip. Small shoulder bag.

USHERS: Black 1985 double-breasted three-piece tuxedo, cotton-polyester blend. White pleated tuxedo shirts with white ruffle dickey with red trim. This ties the usher's design into that of the bridesmaid's. Black patent leather shoes (different in design from Tony) and black socks. ACCESSORIES: red carnation boutonnieres. BARRY: silver ring, optional earring. DOM and JOHNNY: crucifix, ring optional.

BRIDESMAIDS: One-shouldered red rayon crepe dress. Fitted lace-covered bodice with a full skirt hemmed just below the knee with a scalloped lace edging. Red rayon crepe bow attached at the left shoulder. Red lace fingerless gloves to the wrist. ACCESSORIES: One or two pieces of distinctive jewelry. All should choose the pantyhose their characters demand, but only in red. Shoes do not have to be of the same style, but should match the red of the dresses. BRIDESMAIDS SHOULD NEVER WEAR THEATRICAL DANCE SHOES.

JOEY: Subtle black pin-stripe single-breasted two piece tuxedo. Bright red shiny cummerbund with matching bow tie. White wing-tip tuxedo shirt, black jazz shoes with red socks. Red rose for the lapel. ACCESSORIES: gold bracelet and ring, optional earring. NOTE: It is important that the white stripes on his tuxedo not be prominent. If a subtle pin-stripe tuxedo cannot be found, a solid black single-breasted tuxedo is the best second choice.

UNCLE LUIGI: All of Uncle Luigi's clothes are vintage. The jacket and pants shouldn't quite match. The entire outfit should be about two sizes too big. Pants: dark brown, thick gabardine. Preferably 1940's style. Belt: old, but in good shape. Jacket: 100% cotton, also brown tones. Shirt: 100% cotton, light baby blue, long-sleeved. Hat: 1960's "Bing Crosby" style, blue-brown weave with small feather. Certainly not dressy enough for the occasion. Tie: vintage 1940's wide, with simple but subtle Italian picture or scene (a gondola, etc.) Socks: thick white sweat socks or gym-socks (for his swollen feet). Shoes: one pair crisscross vinyl sandals; one pair black pull-on rubber rain boots. ACCESSORIES: cane, hearing-aid, gold ring, white handkerchief. NOTES ON UNCLE LUIGI: Uncle Luigi has shrunk over the years and his clothes should reflect this fact. They are worn and well-used, but they are his favorite dress pieces saved for special occasions, and he picked them out himself.

SISTER ALBERT MARIA: Traditional 100% polyester nun's habit with headpiece. Optional long or short sleeve. Dress length should be one inch below the knee. Black knee-high stockings and plain black "sensible" leather pumps. ACCESSORIES: large black wooden rosary pinned at the hip, silver chain with silver and turquoise crucifix (without Christ figure). NOTES ON SISTER: The fact that Sister is wearing knee-highs should not be noticeable as she stands. It should only become apparent as she begins to dance, twirl and "loosen up." Under no circumstances should Sister wear any make-up whatsoever!

ROSE: Elegant purple and mustard silk blouse with mustard silk slacks (elastic band at the waist). Mustard shoes. Accessories: gold clutch bag, long gold and pearl necklace. Additional necklaces of various colored glass. Matching earrings and rings.

MRS. VITALE: Black lace beaded dress, hemmed four inches below the knee. Very elegant but conservative. Black sheer stockings, black shoes (preferably beaded). ACCESSORIES: gold coin clip on earrings, necklace with single gold coin pendant. Gold charm bracelet for one wrist and various gold bracelets for the other. Three carat diamond ring (Vito's gift for their twenty-fifth anniversary), five carat amethyst ring encircled by diamonds for other hand. She has retrieved from the safe deposit box all the best jewelry that Mr. Vitale gave her over the years. She carries a black beaded clutch-purse.

NUNZIO: Black single-breasted two piece tuxedo with satin lapel. White tuxedo shirt, standard collar (not wing tip). Black bow tie, cummerbund, socks and shoes (patent leather optional). ACCESSORIES: gold watch and ring, red rose boutonniere.

MADELINE: Gold lamé low-cut sleeveless dress. Dress should be at least six inches above the knee with a slit up the back. Should appear to be too tight (remembering that the actress must be able to move freely). There should be a strong, easily managed zipper in the back of at least eighteen inches in length. Black sheer stockings with garter belt. Black spike heels. Black opaque underpants and sturdy black padded bra with lace. ACCESSORIES: gold hoop earrings, bracelets, and rings. NOTES ON MADELINE: Her dress should look cheap, tacky and store-bought. You should look at her and be able to say "I've seen that dress before." However, the dress should accentuate Madeline's complete confidence and awareness of her sexuality.

GRANDMA NUNZIO: Simple, solid black, long-sleeved button-front dress with collar. Rayon, if possible. *Two sizes too big*. Black veil. Black opaque stockings or tights, black Oxford shoes. ACCESSORIES: black vintage purse with strap or handle, antique brooch at the neck, vintage floral shawl for color. [NOTE: All skin except her face and hands should be covered.]

MICHAEL JUST: Worn-out straight-leg jeans, brown suede Wallaby shoes, white socks. Plain baby blue cotton shirt. Red bandanna. No accessories. [NOTE: Michael should look as if he spent the night in the back of his van and slept in his clothes.]

FATHER MARK: Traditional priest's clerical garb. Black shirt, slacks and socks. Black soft leather, spongy rubber-soled shoes. ACCESSORIES: priest's robe for ceremony optional.

VINNIE BLACK: Black single-breasted tuxedo (different from Mr. Nunzio's in design). Deep purple cummerbund and bow-tie. White tuxedo shirt, standard collar (no wing tip). Black patent leather shoes, black silk socks. ACCESSORIES: thick gold chain with Cadillac emblem for his neck, pinkie ring, gold watch. [NOTE: Vinnie should look like a flashy entertainer in a cheap Las Vegas lounge.]

LORETTA BLACK: Vintage 1950's black chiffon *cocktail* dress with *full* chiffon skirt, length just above the knee. Vintage 1950's black pumps with sheer nude stockings. ACCESSORIES: simple bracelet and wedding band. 1950's stone or glass earrings (clip-on), modest diamond-heart necklace. [NOTE: Loretta is not '50's chic. She simply hasn't left the Coliseum in forty years. Her make-up tells the story—it is always applied by lounge-light.

CATERERS: (MALE) Gold Bolero waiters' jackets with "Coliseum" embroidered in burgundy on the left front. Black tuxedo pants with white wing-tip tuxedo shirt. Black bow-tie, shoes and socks. ACCESSORIES: gold metal name tags. *This is absolutely the only accessory for the caterers.*

CATERERS: (FEMALE) Same as the men except black skirt instead of pants. Simple black work shoes and nude panty hose. ACCESSORIES: *simple* earrings, a bracelet, ring, etc.

RICK DeMARCO: Trendy rayon slacks, trendy rayon shirt with design, trendy gabardine jacket. Dress shoes and socks. Accessories optional. [NOTE: Rick is very appropriately dressed for the wedding, but with a gay flair. If you can get a copy of the *International Male* clothing catalog, it will help.]

SAL ANTONUCCI: Vintage 1975 black tuxedo, with black velvet collar. Vintage '70's teal tuxedo shirt with ruffled chest and cuffs. '70's large red satin bow-tie. Black worn out leather shoes with navy blue socks. Accessories: gold bracelet and pinky ring. [NOTE: This is obviously Sal's work tuxedo.]

DONNY DULCE AND FUSION
DONNY: Trendy black Bolero jacket, matching high-waist slacks. White tuxedo shirt, open to the waist. Black and silver waist sash. Black ankle length cowboy boots.

CELESTE ROMANO: Trendy black very fitted, very sexy cocktail dress, preferably one shoulder. Nude stockings, black high heels. Wild accessories; earrings, bracelets, etc.

THE BAND: Silver tuxedos. White tuxedo shirts, different from rest of cast. Accessories optional.

SCENTS

Because of the reality base of the show, and the proximity of the audience to the characters, scents play a part that should be recognized, and indeed exploited. For example, Mrs. Vitale wears "Giorgio of Beverly Hills," Madeline wears "Charlie" and Tina wears "L'Aimant" by Coty. Grandma and Uncle Luigi have that faint odor of old mothballs. A lot can be told about a character by the way they smell.

TROUBLESHOOTING

The improvisational nature of "Tony n' Tina's Wedding" is one of it's greatest assets. However, the freedom and necessity to constantly create brings with it a tendency to overdo. Too much make-up or too many accessories can actually begin to overwhelm the character and ultimately corrupt the proper focus of the play. Always be true to the character, and true to the circumstance—after all, this is "Tony and Tina's Wedding." It is the costumer's responsibility to keep actors in check. Don't be afraid to pull them back to reality.

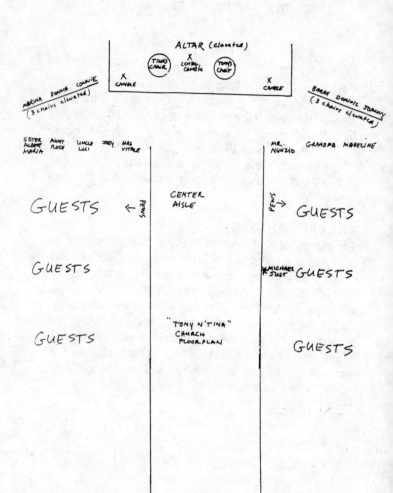

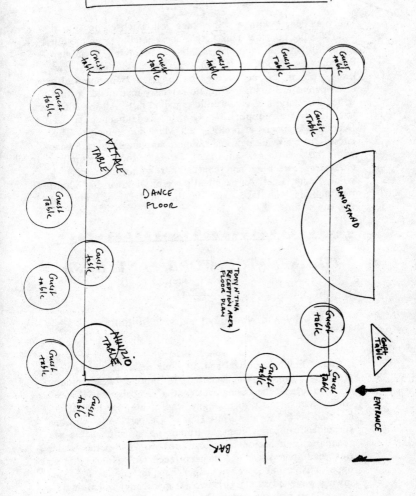

WHAT THE BELLHOP SAW
(Little Theatre)
(FARCE)

by Wm. Van Zandt and Jane Milmore

8 male, 4 female

The play starts with a rather nice fellow checking into a $400.00 suite in "New York City's finest hotel". From there it snowballs into a fabulous nightmare involving a Salman Rushdie-type author, an Iranian Terrorist, a monstrous shrew-like woman, a conniving bellboy, a monumentally incompetent F.B.I. man, a nubile celebrity-mad maid, a dim-witted secretary, and a cute little pigtailed girl. All the while, gag lines are popping at Orville Redenbacher speed. Everything happens at pretty much whirlwind velocity. This latest farce by Van Zandt and Milmore combines topical humor with the traditional antics of farce: doors slamming, characters careening and confusion reigning supreme. A wildly funny farce! An excellent piece of workmanship by our two authors who take pride in the old-fashioned craft of comedy writing. #25062

THE SENATOR WORE PANTYHOSE
(Little Theatre)
(COMEDY)

by Wm. Van Zandt and Jane Milmore

7 male, 3 female

If you're tired of political and religious scandals, this is your greatest revenge! Van Zandt & Milmore's latest comedy revolves around the failing Presidential campaign of "Honest" Gabby Sandalson, a regular guy whose integrity has all but crippled his bid for the White House. Desparate for votes, his sleazeball campaign manager trumps up an implausible sex scandal which accidentally backfires on PMS Club leader Reverend Johnny and his makeup-faced wife Honey Pie; an opportunistic innkeeper with a penchant for antique food; the town's wayward single girl; two escaped convicts looking for stolen loot; and newscaster Don Bother. "A guaranteed hit!" (Asbury Park Press) "The characters swap beds, identities and jabs in what may be a flawless sex farce." (The Register). #21084

MIXED FEELINGS
(Little Theatre—Comedy)

Donald Churchill
m., 2 f., Int.

This is a riotous comedy about divorce, that ubiquitous, peculiar institution which so shapes practically everyone's life. Arthur and Norma, ex-spouses, live in separate apartments in the same building. Norma has second thoughts about her on-going affair with Arthur's best-friend; while Arthur isn't so sure he wants to continue *his* dalliance with Sonia, wife of a manufacturer with amusingly kinky sexual tastes (Dennis—the manufacturer—doesn't mind that his wife is having an affair; just so long as she continues to provide him with titillating accounts of it while he is dressed as a lady traffic cop). Most of Sonia's accounts are pure fiction, which seems to keep Dennis happy. Comic sparks are ignited into full-fledged farcical flames in the second act, when Dennis arrives in Arthur's flat for lessons in love from the legendary Arthur! "Riotous! A domestic laught romp! A super play. You'll laugh all the way home, I promise you.'—Eastbourne News. "Very funny ... a Churchill comedy that most people will thoroughly enjoy."—The Stage. Restricted New York City.

THE DECORATOR
(Little Theatre/Comedy)

Donald Churchill
m., 2 f., Int.

Much to her surprise, Marcia returns home to find that her flat has not been painted, as she arranged. In fact, the job hasn't even been started yet. There on the premises is the housepainter who is filling in for his ill colleague. As he begins work, there is a surprise visitor--the wife of the man with whom Marcia is having an affair, who has come to confront her nemesis and to exact her revenge by informing Marcia's husband of his wife's infidelity. Marcia is at her wit's end about what to do, until she gets a brilliant idea. It seems the housepainter is a part-time professional actor. Marcia hires him to impersonate her husband, Reggie, at the big confrontation later that day, when the wronged wife plans to return and spill the beans. Hilarity is piled upon hilarity as the housepainter, who takes his acting *very* seriously, portrays the absent Reggie. The wronged wife decides that the best way to get back at Marcia would be to sleep with her "husband" (the house painter), which is an ecstatic experience for them both. When Marcia learns that the housepainter/actor/husband has slept with her rival, she demands to have the opportunity to show the housepainter what *really* good sex is. "This has been the most amazing day of my life", says the sturdy painter, as Marcia leads him into her bedroom. "Irresistible."—London Daily Telegraph.

LEND ME A TENOR
(Farce)
by KENNETH LUDWIG

4 male, 4 female

This is the biggest night in history of the Cleveland Grand Opera Company, for this night in September, 1934, world-famous tenor Tito Morelli (also known as "Il Stupendo") is to perform his greatest role ("Otello") at the gala season-opening benefit performance which Mr. Saunders, the General Manager, hopes will put Cleveland on the operatic map. Morelli is late in arriving--and when he finally sweeps in, it is too late to rehearse with the company. Through a wonderfully hilarious series of mishaps, Il Stupendo is given a double dose of tranquilizers which, mixed with all the booze he has consumed, causes him to pass out. His pulse is so low that Saunders and his assistant, Max, believe to their horror that he has died. What to do? What to do? Max is an aspiring singer, and Saunders persuades him to black up, get into Morelli's Otello costume, and try to fool the audience into thinking that's Il Stupendo up there. Max succeeds admirably, but the comic sparks really fly when Morelli comes to and gets into his other costume. Now we have *two* Otellos running around, in costume, and two women running around, in lingerie -- each thinking she is with Il Stupendo! A sensation on Broadway and in London's West End. "A jolly play."--NY Times. "Non-stop laughter"--Variety. "Uproarious! Hysterical!"--USA Today. "A rib-tickling comedy."--NY Post. (#667) **Posters.**

POSTMORTEM
(Thriller)
by KENNETH LUDWIG

4 male, 4 female . Int..

Famous actor-manager and playwright William Gillette, best known for over a generation as Sherlock Holmes in his hugely-successful adaptation of Conan Doyle (which is *still* a popular play in the Samuel French Catalogue), has invited the cast of his latest revival of the play up for a weekend to his home in Connecticut, a magnificent pseudo-medieval, Rhenish castle on a bluff overlooking the Connecticut River. Someone is trying to murder William Gillette, and he has reason to suspect that it is one of his guests for the weekend. Perhaps the murderer is the same villain who did away with Gillette's fiancee a year ago if you believe, as does Gillette, that her death was not--as the authorities concluded--a suicide. Gillette's guests include his current ingenue/leading lady and her boyfriend, his Moriarty and his wife, and Gillette's delightfully acerbic sister. For the evening's entertainment Gillette has arranged a seance, conducted by the mysterious Louise Perradine, an actress twenty years before but now a psychic medium. The intrepid and more than slightly eccentric William Gillette has taken on, in "real life", his greatest role: he plans to solve the case *a la* Sherlock Holmes! The seance is wonderfully eerie, revealing one guest's closely-guarded secret and sending another into hysterics, another into a swoon, as Gillette puts all the pieces of the mystery together before the string of attempts on his life leads to a rousingly melodramatic finale. " shots in the dark and darkly held secrets, deathbed letters, guns and knives and bottles bashed over the head, ghosts and hiders behind curtains and misbegotten suspicions. There are moments when you'll jump. Guaranteed."--The Telegraph. (#18677)